W9-AHY-780

DATE DUE			
FE1 '96			
MAY 15			
JUN 29			

BOWHUNTER

BOWHUNTER

Stephen Altman

Walker and Company
New York

First published in the United States of America in 1988
by the Walker Publishing Company, Inc.

Published simultaneously in Canada by Thomas Allen & Son
Canada, Limited, Markham, Ontario.

Library of Congress Cataloging-in-Publication Data

Altman, Stephen, 1950–
  Bowhunter / Stephen Altman.
    p.   cm.
  ISBN 0-8027-4085-5
  I. Title.
PS3551.L794B69   1988   813'.54—dc19   88-15620

Printed in the United States of America

10 9 8 7 6 5 4 3 2 1

For Ellie

Contents

BOWHUNTER

Part 1

Out of Dodge

CHAPTER 1

THE night me and Uncle Noah and Bill Nunan were in the Lady Gay, the girls were up on the stage doing the cancan. There was enough cigar smoke so's you couldn't hardly see nor breathe, and enough music and shouting and laughter so's you couldn't hardly hear. Most of the fellers that weren't wrapped up in poker or faro games were banging their glasses on the bar and hollering for more liquor or for the girls to hitch their skirts up higher. Across the table from me, Jim Fitch said something about my Pa. What with all the commotion in there, I couldn't be certain I'd heard him right.

"Want to say that again for me?"

Fitch leaned forward over the cards and the money and the bottles and glasses—close enough for me to smell his breath.

"What I said was, I said your pa was crazier than hell. I said I whupped him like a dog, and I'll whup his son, too."

This time I heard him.

It was a shame that when a feller got to Dodge he had to check his guns—for I would rather have shot Jim Fitch right there than have had to bare-knuckle it with him. At nineteen I was as tall as I'd ever get—every bit of six-foot-one, and taller in boots—but I hadn't yet filled out. Jim Fitch was put together more substantial—big and hairy and slope-shouldered, like he should be pulling a wagon.

I hit him anyway. It was a good bust in the jaw, considering that I was sitting down when I threw it. When it landed it felt solid. I had high hopes for it.

What it did was, it made him smile.

3

"You got sand, boy."

"I got more'n that if you'll come out from back of there."

He come round the table right quick for one his size and cuffed me on the ear just as I was raising out of my chair. I crashed backwards onto the floor.

Time slowed some down there in the sawdust. Fitch come back into focus and I saw him reach into his belt for a leather quirt. It weren't no ordinary quirt, but one of the long and mean-looking variety that the bad ones fill with lead shot. I'd seen men bust a horse with that sort of thing—just whaling at it betwixt the ears each time it would act up, till the horse was either tame or dead.

Jim Fitch swung that quirt around, taking time to build up some steam, and when he'd got up a full head he let out a rebel yell. Had this been seventeen years previous and we were at Shiloh together, it might have been nice to have a wailer like that on your side. But tonight that howl scared me half to death.

It was still going on when he dove for me. He was in midair when I shot the heel of my boot into his crotch. The rebel yell changed pitch as he passed overhead. The quirt clattered off somewheres.

Somebody in the crowd said, "Like your style, boy."

We were both up pretty quick, and Fitch was hot. The look in his eyes was different now. He charged again, waving his big right fist about head-high like a club. I ducked—and his left was waiting. It struck my jaw but I felt it in the back of my head. He poked me hard in the eyes, and when my hands went to squinch down on them he plowed his right hand into my belly and doubled me over. I was on my way down when he brung his knee up like a piston and rattled my teeth.

So now I was on the floor again, tasting blood and wanting only to die or hide somewhere, but knowing that things would only get worse if I didn't get up right quick. I managed to unfold myself and my vision started to clear. He still stood there—whiskered and ugly and gloating on me.

So I smiled and said, "Come get it, you dumb son of a bitch."

This time he charged with his head down. I sidestepped him and got an arm locked round his neck. He tried to shake me off and we hopped through a dance step or two, and then we crashed into the bar. Bottles and beer glasses hit the floor and then so did we, knocking over a full spittoon as we did. I mashed his face down into the slop—which brung me some small amount of pleasure but didn't harm him none—and pretty soon with those powerful shoulders of his, he twisted free.

Then I saw the quirt. It was laying just across the floor, not ten feet distant from us. Fitch saw it too and tried to get up and make a dash for it, but slipped on spit and spilled beer and went tumbling forward. I picked up a chair and brung it down on his head.

And then, for a wonder, all the whistling and cheering stopped. I waited on him to see if he'd stir. But he just laid there by the spittoon.

Noah stepped over him and took aholt of me. "Well, son, looks like old Fitch met a chair he couldn't lick."

I might have made answer to that, but everything begun to spin round on me real slow, and I felt like I might like to rest.

What had led up to it was this. . . . A bunch of us had drove a herd into Kansas by way of the Great Western Trail. Twenty-six hundred steers, three months trailing up from Corpus Christi, $112 a man. When we coaxed the last steer into the pens by the railroad, the job was done, so me and Uncle Noah and another hand name of Bill Nunan rode the five miles into Dodge to draw our time and rid ourselves of as much of our wages as we could.

We got bathed and shaved and headed for the Lady Gay. We'd heard this was Dodge's finest dance hall, which we understood to mean that we could find all manner of wickedness there without having to hunt further.

The last time I'd been to Dodge was five years previous, when I was fourteen. Pa and me had been two years on the buffalo range. We'd made sacks of money, and by that time the newspapermen from back East had begun to write about Pa so that folks from all over knew the name Bowhunter. There were dime novels with him in it, like "King of the Buffalo Men," and you'd find mention of me in there, too. We made a team—Micah Bowhunter and son.

But one day, sitting on a bench along the sidewalk right here in Dodge, Pa said he'd asked around and there was this school in New Orleans that would make a gentleman out of me and he said, "Tory, when that train leaves here tomorrow morning, you'll be on it."

I was, and it was the last I seen him.

About a year after I went off to school, Pa disappeared. Ceased taking hides, they said. Got drunk a lot and fought considerable. Then he lit out. No one had heard from him since.

No one, that is, till that night at the Lady Gay.

Me and Noah and Bill had been playing poker, and we'd been doing right well. Most of this was at Jim Fitch's expense. Fitch was a local operator who was used to taking money from cowpunchers. We were beating him bad. It made him surly.

Late into the evening our trail boss walks in with a letter for me. He says it's been forwarded to Dodge from Corpus Christi. Been setting at the post office for more than a month. I opened it up and this is what it said:

10 June 1879

Dear Tory Boy—

Yr needed here. Important you arrive at
first pos. instant.

Sincrly yrs,
Micah Bowhunter (yr pa)

That made its impression on me. I must have read it over about ten times before I handed it to Noah.

"Tourmaline," he said. "Tourmaline, Colorado."

"What?" It was loud in there.

"I said, Tourmaline, Colorado. Says so right here. Micah's someplace called Tourmaline."

"Where's that at?"

He didn't look like he knew. But suddenly Bill Nunan said, "Your pa's found gold!"

"Huh?"

Nunan leaned across the feller next to him and shouted. "Tory boy, ain't but one reason a feller heads for Colorado—to find gold. He must've hit it big to be so mysterious about it."

I thought that over. But meantime Bill had more to say.

"First you got Bowhunter the buffalo man—now it's Bowhunter the millionaire!"

I was still kind of in a daze. All of a sudden Fitch brings his fist down on the table.

"Bowhunter?" he says. "Micah Bowhunter?"

"Yessir," I said. "I'm Tory Bowhunter, his son."

That's when Jim Fitch said something about Pa that I didn't quite make out. And that's how the fight started. . . .

I wakened in a bed—something pleasurous to a man who's been sleeping on the ground for three months. It's been my experience that a comfortable bed will provide more consolation than a woman in most cases, and in the long run is less troublesome.

There was a woman setting alongside me—dabbing at my face with a doily or somesuch.

I said, "What is that stuff?"

She said, "It's rosewater, honey. Do you like it?"

Saloon sounds were coming through the wall, and men and women were laughing in the hallway. I reasoned it out that we were in one of the rooms back of the Lady Gay.

I said, "How'd I get here?"

She had a laughing way in how she spoke—like a man couldn't ask a question nor tell a lie she hadn't heard before. "Your uncle and that other feller drug you in. They seemed to think I could do more for you than they could. Think I might?"

I inquired of her name.

"Why honey," she said, "I thought all you cowboys carried my picture. I'm Sarie Clement."

"Pleased, ma'am." I was more than pleased. I'd heard of Sarie Clement.

Sarie poured herself a drink. She drunk it and then poured one for me in the same glass. "I've told you who I am," she said. "Who are you?"

Just as sweet as could be, she settled in kinda languid beside me and poured herself another shot.

I told her my name was Tory Bowhunter—and that stopped her cold.

"You're kin to Micah?"

"His son, ma'am."

She got up off the bed—my heart sank—and brung the lamp over. She peered at me and I peered at her. I'm forced to say that bright lights didn't much flatter her. Her skin seemed thin as paper and as blanched as the buffalo bones we'd seen stacked out by the railroad tracks.

"Yes, you're Micah's, all right," she said. "I can see him in you. Same dark eyes. Some of your mother, too. She was Mexican, wasn't she?"

"Yes'm. How did you know that?"

"I knew your pa. Is he doin' good?"

"I can't say. All I've heard is he's in Colorado. I'm fixin' to find him, though."

She sighed. "That was some man." She set back down on the bed again—but this time there weren't nothing professional about it. I could tell she was settling in just to talk.

"You know," she said, "when Micah would get to town he'd come here first? To this very room. The man they wrote books about." She sighed again. "All of Dodge would be buzzin' over him, but he'd come right to me. Walk in here big as life, with his buffalo mange and his buckskins all full of blood and old sweat—and I'd bathe him with a big soft sponge and put out clean sheets for him to lay on and, well— he was gentle, you know. Afterwards we'd, well, talk, like we was friends. Just like friends."

She kind of leaned over and brushed the hair from my forehead. It made me feel funny—good, though. It was a dreamy sort of thing—like when I was a boy, before Ma's passing.

Her eyes were far off somewhere. "Did you know he got to hatin' it—all the killing? Folks thought he'd gone soft, said he was talkin' loco—but it weren't like that. He just quit is all. Went to Colorado to look for gold." Her eyes come back to me. "You say he's still out there?"

"That's how I heard it, ma'am. But I can't say where, exactly."

"He lit out with some old Dutchman he met. Wolf some- thin'—Muller, Miller, somethin' like that. One night your pa set up drinking with him and the next day they left. He said good-bye and I never seen him again."

"When was that?"

"A little more'n four years. That's the last anybody in Dodge seen him."

I pondered that. Pa sent me off in the summer of 1874. He give up everything in the summer of 1875. Somewhere during that year he'd changed.

Well, it was all still a mystery. But this Muller or Miller or whoever he was, gave me one thing I didn't have before—a name to inquire after when I got beyond the Rockies.

Sarie fetched forth another bottle and poured for us. She talked about herself, pausing now and again to cough like an old woman and soothe it with whiskey. She told me she hoped to stay in Dodge, told me how they'd already run her out of Abilene and Caldwell on account of men kept fighting over her. Something about her, she said, made men want not to share.

I said, "Did ya ever try settlin' in with just one?"

She put her hand on mine and said, "Honey, it just seemed like it would have been such a waste."

I liked that woman. She made up for being all broke down by being so sweet-spoken. The more I drank the more I felt right tender toward her, and I wanted to get to know her better but I passed out.

Next I know, somebody's pounding on the door like the place is afire.

"You makin' progress in there, Tory boy?"

I leaped up. Sarie said, "That's Noah."

Outside the door that voice bellowed. "None other, Sarie girl. You mistreatin' that boy?"

She was in no shape to mistreat nobody. Maybe I was more sober than I'd been, and maybe daylight was cruel to her, but she looked even worse this morning than she did the night before. She sprawled there in her chair like she was worn out. The saddest part was the little smile she give me.

Noah was hollering, "Come on out here, Tory boy. Help me get my pants on!"

I said to Sarie, "Did you get any sleep?"

She shook her head and waved a hand over at the two empty bottles. "Tried to."

I looked at her. "I gotta go."

It weren't even late morning but we run into Bill Nunan at the bar. He was a good-looking man, with the sort of hard, straight features I might've wisht for. I look more pug-Mexican. We didn't know each other that good. I knew him for a good hand on a cattle drive, though a mite showy for my taste.

"How about a drink, fellers?" he called out.

"Thanks, but no, Bill," I said. "We're gonna buy us some breakfast, load 'er up, and then we're gone."

Nunan raised his glass. "Gone for gold in the wild, wild Rockies," he said. "Takes a special breed of man. A man as rough and tumble as the land itself."

"You read too many books," Noah said.

Just then one of the dance hall gals come up to tell me that Sarie wanted to see me. I left Noah and Bill at the bar.

When I got to her room, she said, "I wrote out somethin' for your pa. I'd be obliged if you'd pass it along to him."

I took the envelope from her. She placed her hand on top of mine. "You're gonna find him?"

I said, "He's expecting me."

She smiled. "I owe you some favors when you come back."

I went back downstairs. Me and Noah had one last beer with Nunan, but I didn't say much. I was thinking about Sarie Clement in that little room of hers. Then we headed across the plaza to the livery stable. I slung the packsaddle over the mule and double-cinched 'er while Noah saddled his horse. Then as I saddled my horse Temper, I told Noah about Sarie and Pa.

I said, "I wonder how much he give up when he left here. I hadn't ever thought of Pa being lonesome or nothing. But I'll bet everyone gets loncsome, don't they?"

It was shady in the stables so I couldn't hardly see Noah's eyes. But they were on me.

He said, "You get older, son, you grow accustomed to it. It's like the dust that blows in under the door. There ain't no gettin' away from it."

"And it don't stop?"

"It don't stop."

CHAPTER 2

IN three days me and Uncle Noah had covered a hundred miles of western Kansas and were feeling pretty good—hot but good. It was late in the day and we were following a creek that looked like a place to make camp. But the urge was on us just to make a few more miles while the daylight remained.

It was rolling country—plenty of deep blue sky overhead, lots of room for seeing—and all around us on the hills and ridges the grass stood shimmering, and in the hollows between them the earth had begun to cool as the darkness gathered.

Out of one of them hollows come six Indians on horseback. First we heard them. Then as they come up over the ridge we saw the rifles they were waving over their heads, and then their faces, and then their mounts. The sun lit 'em up like torches.

"Look at that," Noah said. "Six of the real article."

Sure looked real. Near to naked far as I could tell, whoopin' it up right serious, shaking their Winchesters and galloping hard for us.

We spun the horses round toward the creek with the thought to gain some cover amongst the cottonwoods. I was up on the bay horse, tugging Temper and Noah's paint behind. Noah had the mule in tow—which didn't put up no fuss or nothing but slowed us some. Slowed or not, we weren't gonna shake those Indians. A loaded-up pack mule was just the sort of prize these Indians were after.

We knew we weren't gonna make it to the trees. The whoops were getting closer. Lead was popping overhead and it was only a matter of time till one of us caught a hunk of it.

There was too much noise for us to hear each other, but Noah pointed for me to follow him over to the westward. He must've caught sight of something. Then I saw it—a buffalo wallow, one of them lovely round holes buffalo used to dig to take baths in the dirt. Time after time, one after another, the buffalo had rubbed their humps against the earth— ending up with a sloping hole in the ground so big that years later two men could use it to fight off Indians.

And it was a big hole—the biggest wallow I ever saw. We spurred 'em to it and our whole outfit tumbled in. Then me and Noah were up against the rim, giving them Indians nothing much to shoot at but two hats and a lot of white smoke.

We had to make our first shots count because pretty soon them braves would be circling, firing into us from all sides. Coming straight on they made poor targets, but at least we could face them all at once. I took aim on the leader and knocked his horse down. But the Indian didn't miss a beat. He hit the ground running straight at us, his victory howl coming up from deep inside him so's you knew he felt pretty good about his chances. Twenty yards off he raised his Winchester to fire and Noah shot him dead.

In the meantime I took out the next rider. Couldn't tell where I hit him, but the jolt spun him all the way around and he hit the ground facing the way he come. His friends swung around to our right.

I could hear Noah say, "Well, I'll be."

"How's that?"

"These here is Comanches," he shouted. "This far north Comanches is a rarity."

They were yip-yipping something fierce, firing all the while. Suddenly, one of them Comanches—pony and all— flew over the rim and into the wallow with us.

The stock went loco, pounding around in a circle. The Indian pony joined in, all of them whinnying with fear, kicking up dust so's you couldn't see an arm's length in front of you. Problem was, somewhere in that cloud of dust was a Comanche.

"I'll take him," I said, and ventured into it.

But he was behind me. He had a forearm clamped round my chest and the hand with the knife was coming up under my chin. I snapped my head back into his face and he let go, but as I spun around the blade gouged me along the chin. I saw him then—and damn but he was bloodier than I was. When I'd thrown back my head I must've broke his nose, and as he raised his hand to feel it I grabbed his other hand with the knife in it and brung it around and into his gut.

That's three, I thought. I called out "Noah!" but with the horses in a commotion and shots still ringing I didn't know if he'd hear. I sure couldn't hear him. Worse yet, I'd lost my Winchester when that brave latched onto me. All I could do was pull the Indian's blade out of his belly and go looking for my uncle.

It was barely a frog's jump to the yon side of the wallow, but when I caught sight of Noah I was just too far from him. He and a brave were tangling—Noah with his knife in hand and the brave in close, using his Winchester for a club. The Indian hit him a blow to the hand that sent the knife up onto the rim alongside him. You could see Noah weighing whether to reach for it. He got his arm extended and the brave smashed his rifle butt down through Noah's elbow. There was a cracking sound and the arm snapped the wrong way. Then the Indian swung the rifle butt around into Noah's jaw and he went down—and just as that happened the horses cut between us and I couldn't do nothing but stand there.

It felt like I was trapped for an hour whilst the horses hustled by—and when they were past I saw Noah facedown in the whirling dust with that Indian straddling him. The brave had Noah's hair in one hand, yanking Noah's head back, and was bringing his blade across with the other.

I don't think my feet hit the ground but I was on him, and I had my steel in that Comanche's throat before he could get that blade halfway home. I took the Indian's shoulders in both my hands and tore him off Noah's back, and I stomped him with my boot. But it was no time to lose sight of other things. For whilst I took out my rage and my fear on a dead Indian, over my shoulder one of the live ones let out a cry and leapt from the rim.

I wasn't gonna give up. It might be I was choking on dust and blood and had nothing left to fight with but my hands— but by God I could still strangle a man. As he dropped down onto me I ducked so's he'd land on my back. I bent even further to flip him over my head, but something didn't feel right. He felt less like a live Indian than a sack of flour.

Turned out there was good reason for that. Someone had shot him in midair. From behind.

And over the rim, Bill Nunan stuck in his head and said, "Howdy."

There was no moving Noah since night was falling, so we made camp in the switchgrass alongside the wallow. I went to retrieve my Winchester and almost fell over the sixth Comanche, laying there in the grass with one of Noah's bullets in his chest, eyes wide open, gazing up like he was still alive. I squatted by him. He'd been a strong man, lean as a wolf, with hard, proud features. He had copper bands on his arms, old knife scars crisscrossing his chest. This one had been tested more than once, and he'd taken as good as he'd given—you knew that. I closed his eyelids for him and drug his body over by the others.

Bill and me got the stock out of the wallow, settled them down, and got some pegs drove in the ground to hitch them to for the night. There were plenty of buffalo chips laying about for a fire. We tried to get some hot beans into Noah but he was sick to his stomach. He was sweating fierce. When I spoke to him he didn't answer. His face was swelled up where he was struck, and he'd been bleeding considerable inside his mouth.

His arm, though, was what fretted me. I'd never before seen a man's broken bones jutting through the skin. I pushed them back in with my fingers, and the flesh after them. I wiped away the blood and dirt and poured whiskey onto the wound and wrapped it and tried not to let on that I saw the tears running out of Noah's eyes.

I trickled some water into my bandanna and wiped his face real gentle-like. All the while I kept talking to him, telling him how he would mend right quick, and how the Comanche that hurt him was in plenty worse shape than he was. And I told him how Bill Nunan had showed up and taken out the last of those braves, so that amongst us we'd killed all six and there'd be a heap of burying to do in the morning.

Before he slept I took the length of horsehair rope from Noah's saddle and laid it down in a circle around him to keep off snakes. I reckoned then that I'd done all I could.

I squatted down by the fire and set to thinking. Noah was in need of a doctor. There was none back in Dodge. Denver would be the place.

So I concluded that we'd head north. The Kansas-Pacific line run east-west across the northern part of the state. If we got to the tracks and could flag a westbound train, we'd be in Denver in a couple of days. That would give us a good shot at getting Noah patched up, and would get us a sight closer to where we were headed in the first place.

Bill had rustled up some jerky and hardtack to go with the beans. I brung up the notion of flagging a train.

He looked a mite unsure about it. "You're just gonna go out there and stand in front of a locomotive?"

"Yessir."

"Just like that."

"That's right."

Bill kinda shrugged his shoulders. I got up to fetch some tobacco from my saddle. I didn't know why Bill Nunan had been trailing us a hundred miles out of Dodge. I was more than half glad he'd done it, but I wisht I knew what he was up to. The worst it could be, I reckoned, was that he wanted in on Pa's gold and was hoping we'd take him with us. I didn't mind it. Out on the Great Western he'd made a good hand—a little flashy, like I said, but sound. We could use him now, and if it cost us a little gold I reckoned we owed him at least that much anyway.

I said, "You're comin' with us, ain't ya?"

It was full dark by then but in the firelight you could see the flash of his grin.

He said, "Somebody's got to protect you from Comanches."

Truth be told, neither of us reckoned to meet up with any more of them. The Comanche, the Kiowa, the Kiowa-Apache—they were hemmed up now in the Indian Territory, living on whatever crumbs the white man happened to throw in their direction. By treaty they couldn't hunt north of the Arkansas. We reckoned the bunch we'd tangled with had taken their chances—fording the river a safe distance west of Fort Dodge, and then searching to the northward for buffalo. They must have been pretty desperate. In my mind's eye I could see them riding, mile upon mile on the grasslands, coming to realize in due time that there was just nothing left. By that juncture, two lonely pilgrims like me and Noah must have looked pretty good to them.

Now they were dead. I tallied it up for both sides. Uncle Noah was all busted up. We had us a spotted Comanche pony. And for the first time in my life I'd killed a man— three men. I turned my thoughts aside.

I checked the stock, Temper especially, and set down nearby, resting my Winchester across my knees. It was easy to see a far piece out there, with the moon riding high and bright up yonder. Easy for your thoughts to roam, too. The wind on my face felt like a woman's hand.

I thought about women then, and how I'd hardly knowed any—save for a señorita or two down by Corpus Christi. It seemed that women would be worth knowing, given time. I thought about Pa, too, and how long it had been since me and him rode together, and how it hurt some, not being with him these five years. I reckoned it would be a few more weeks before we got into the high country beyond the Rockies. I knew he was out there under this same sky tonight. I knew that he was guarding that claim of his, that he'd be sure in his heart that I would be there to help out.

It was two o'clock by the stars when I woke Bill and turned in. By first light we'd had coffee and bacon and were breaking ground for our Comanche friends. It wasn't much of a grave we dug, but we got them covered up, and maybe the crows and prairie wolves got them later and maybe they didn't. You felt for 'em less by daylight.

Me and Bill were covering up the last one when Noah roused himself. Half his face was kind of yellow and blue-black, but his jaw worked good enough to take breakfast. He was able to talk now but didn't say nothing concerning his arm. We rigged a sling for it and fetched him up onto the sorrel. We couldn't make a travois on account of we'd need wooden poles for that. There weren't a long skinny tree to be seen from one edge of the sky to the other.

Me and Bill mounted up and I said to Noah, "You ready?"

He said, "If I ain't ready, I'm akin to it."

"Then let's roll 'em."

CHAPTER 3

I RECKON the throb in Noah's arm settled some. He rode good enough so's we could put some miles behind us. We made our nooning among some old willows that fringed a creek where the water run just deep enough to dip your hat. Some quail broke cover nearby and we watched them flutter up and wheel to the westward. As far as a feller could see, the long grass rustled under the wind as gold as wheat.

Bill said, "I'll venture no one's gone over this place for bones."

I said, "Don't see no bones."

"They're in the grass. You got to burn off the grass."

Myself, I didn't see much point in setting a prairie fire just to turn up a few dollars' worth of buffalo bones. I let my eyes wander over the creek. Then it come to me. I knew this place. You don't forget land you've camped on and hunted over, even if you were just a boy of twelve when you did. This here was Punished Woman Fork, running northeasterly to join up with the Smoky Hill River. After the ford it was half a day's ride to the railroad.

Last I'd seen of this location was late in 1872, with Pa. Between 'em, Ma and Uncle Noah'd been trying to make a rancher out of Pa down Corpus Christi way. We lost Ma to the cholera that spring. Pa'd run off two or three times previous and come back on account of her. This time we knew he'd be gone for good.

I asked him to let me tag along. Well, not asked exactly, but moped around so's he'd take the hint. I was a little feller then, but I could already ride like a man, and I'd learned cow so young that people thought I'd been calved instead of born. Pa said I could tag after him on condition he could send me back to Noah whenever he wished to—no questions asked. He joined up with a trail drive headed north on the Chisholm, and talked the drover into taking me on to help tend the remuda.

When we reached Abilene, word was about that there was good money in buffalo hides. A dried, flattened bull hide— what they called a flint—brung $3.50 at the railhead. With the prairie still teeming with buffalo, a man could take down a fair living in that line of work. 'Course, a lot of greenhorns went out to try and came back dead, or near to it. But the ones who managed to dodge Indians and illness and injury and all manner of catastrophe on the plains, and who could shoot straight and outthink buffalo—they did all right.

Now, some men just take to one thing or another better than other men. Pa drew our time at drive's end, got us outfitted and onto the prairie, and found out that he was made to hunt buffalo. He knew how to find them, and he knew how to set up a stand so's they'd stay still, and he knew how to kill 'em in quantity. Weren't long before he had five men working for him, three skinners and two drivers, and had sold off his Remington for something better fitted to the work.

Maybe that's what I recollect clearest from those early days with Pa—the rifle. It was a single-shot, .50 caliber Sharps "Big Fifty" buffalo gun, chambered special for Pa. It took a slug that weighed 700 grains, with 170 grains of black powder behind it in a shellcase more than three inches long. The gun weighed eighteen pounds.

It was an afternoon early in the fall that year when we fetched up on Punished Woman Fork. The outfit made camp and me and Pa went to scout for buffalo. Maybe three miles upstream we found ourselves on a low bluff about two hundred yards south of where the creek flowed.

We shielded our eyes and stared north-by-northwest to the horizon, and what we saw right there was the biggest herd of

buffaloes there's ever been. There weren't no end to them.
A clump of 'em here, a clump of 'em there—mile upon mile
and over the curve of the earth. Bulls and cows with calves
beside them, some grazing, some drifting down to the creek,
some just laying in the grass—and all of it so peaceful, not
like a herd of animals at all—more like an endless forest of
old, old trees.

Pa said, "Son, this here's the promised land."

So we rode to fetch the others. When we got back Pa made
a stand at the edge of the bluff. We were downwind of the
herd, but like as not it didn't much matter, since buffalo
never did learn the scent of white men. Pa set up a forked
shooting stick for resting the barrel of the Sharps, fell down
behind it and drew a bead on a bull by the creekbank. I
watched the old beast and waited on him to drop.

But Pa didn't fire. He got to his feet and motioned me
over.

He said, "Tory boy, this is gonna be a big stand. We're
takin' some hides today. The first one's yours, for good luck."

I was down behind that gun before Pa had a chance to
change his mind. I hefted the stock and took off the trigger
guard. That Sharps was as long as I was. I sighted up a bull.
Pa'd taught me that you aim for the lungs—what he called
the lights—not the heart. A buffalo with a slug in his heart
could run a long ways and get the others to moving as well.
But shoot out the lights and he'd stay home.

I took a breath and held it, then squeezed the trigger.
There was a boom like a cannon and the stock jumped back
at me.

The bull took a step. Blood welled out of his nostrils. Then
his front legs give way. He crumpled forward—like he was
fixing to kneel in prayer—and then he rolled onto his side.
Dust flew up. It was all real slow and stately, like a ship
keeling over.

I blinked and got to my feet and slapped the dust off my

leggin's. Pa give me a long stare. He said, "Son, you're a buffalo hunter." I half expected he'd hug me.

But then he was back on the ground and loading up again. Once the first buffalo was down, a hunter couldn't let the herd commence to thinking. They were none too bright, didn't connect the sound of gunfire with getting blasted. A feller might sneeze and they'd stampede, but fire a boomer like that Big Fifty and they'd just get to milling around. Before long, though, the scent of blood would get on the wind and one or two would grow restive. The hunter had to stay a step ahead of them—making certain the ones that caught on quickest were the first to drop.

The skinners couldn't move in till Pa was done shooting, so them and the drivers squatted round Pa to watch him work. He killed a bull alongside the first one, reloaded, killed another. Then a cow—mostly to clear his line of sight to another old bull behind her.

I kept close by to help out. Every three or four shots I got around front of the rifle and ran a long-stemmed Fisher brush down the bore to clear it of fouled powder.

Pa was going good. They were dropping one after another, so fast the barrel begun to heat up and I had to pour water over it. You could ruin the barrel firing too fast.

He kept at it. One dozen, two dozen—and beyond the creek the live ones just browsed amongst the dead ones till Pa shot them, too. By the time Pa had shot fifty buffaloes, the men knew they were watching something mighty, and still Pa loaded 'er up and fired. I cleaned out the fouled powder and cooled the barrel, and Pa loaded 'er up again.

He'd killed more than his three skinners could skin that day, even if they'd started right then. But he kept going. I heard one of the drivers say, "That's a hundred." One of the skinners, a big red-haired feller, brung over more cartridges. Pa reached into the box without taking his eyes from the herd.

We all gazed at the sight. There was sound a'plenty, but

even with the steady thunder of that Big Fifty, things *felt* quiet. A buffalo would topple, and Pa'd sight up another, and then the next one, boom, in a trance of killing.

Then of a sudden he give it up. Just stood up, stretched, and said, "That'll do 'er."

Now these here skinners and drivers were hardcase buffalo men, and they weren't much given to celebrating on the job. But right then they whooped it up and clapped Pa on the back.

"One hundred seventy-three buffalo," the driver said. "One hour and twenty minutes."

The red-haired skinner said, "Move over, Bill Cody."

Pa said, "Bill Cody, shit. I could've killed the whole herd but I lost interest."

Right there was where Pa made his name. Even later, when he won contests against buffalo men the likes of Billy Dixon and Rawhide Wilson, and even after that when they got to telling tall ones about him shooting a charging bull between the eyes and turning a stampede single-handed—sooner or later they'd get back to that first big stand by the fork that day in 1872.

Two days later the outfit was still skinning Pa's kill and hauling the hides back to camp. I helped the skinners stake the hides out to dry. A green hide might weigh a hundred pounds, but these skinners were big enough that any of them could just flip one out like a bedroll. I drove the pegs and they'd stretch the hides to them, flesh side up. By the time we were done, the staked hides from Pa's stand covered three acres.

The red-haired skinner pulled the bandanna down from his nose and mouth. He said, "Still got your tail?"

"Yessir," I said. Pa'd cut the tail for me off the bull I'd shot. I was prouder'n hell about it.

I packed that tail along nearly two years after, when Pa sent me away. And when I run off from school in New Orleans, I took it on the fishing boat with me. And nearly five years after that, setting there in the shade by Punished Woman Fork, I still had it in my war bag.

By early next morning we made the Kansas-Pacific right-of-way. Due east was a little spot where the tracks came up over the horizon. Due west was the spot where they disappeared again. In between there was nothing but me and Bill and my uncle.

I stared down them tracks and the hours went by and I wondered what the hell ever made me think we could flag down a train. I said, "Supposin' we wave at the engineer and all he does is wave back?"

Uncle Noah said, "No use frettin' over it. Not now."

I asked him why not.

" 'Cause the train's comin'."

Down the tracks to the east, way off through the heat waves, you could see the white smoke pluming.

I hobbled the horses in case they didn't take to the roar of locomotives. All but Temper, who wouldn't be hobbled. I let him stand there. Me and that animal could always reach an agreement—so long as I let him do whatever he pleased.

Trains move right quick on this stretch of rail. The thought come to me that it might have been nice to catch this one on an upgrade. Kind of late for that, though. I calculated that the distance to the nearest upgrade couldn't be more than two hundred miles, due west.

I commenced to hopping up and down on the tracks. The train just kept coming. When the whistle commenced to blow steady I knew the engineer was thinking things over. I just eyeballed him till my legs ached to jump out of the way. I let 'em ache. It got to the point, I reckon, where he just had to yield to his better nature. The steam shot out of the sides of the locomotive. The squealing of the brakes could have made a man deaf.

'Course, a man wouldn't have minded being made deaf if it meant he wouldn't get squashed instead. I jumped aside and let her come to a stop. Temper reared as the engine went by, but mostly he held his ground. Too goddamn mean to give an inch is what he was. I ran after the train and when I come up alongside the cab the engineer had a shotgun pointed at my nose.

Standing between him and the fireman was a fat man in a soft gray suit. He had a white mustache, wore spectacles and a big silk top hat, and with his silver-knobbed cane he looked like the marquis of this or the duke of that.

He said, "I suggest you talk fast, lad."

"My name's Tory Bowhunter, sir. Me and my uncle were headed for Denver, but we got waylaid by Indians and he's too bung up to ride."

He studied me long and scrupulous, like I were a piece of bad handwriting. "You mean you're Micah's boy?"

"Well, yessir, I am."

A big sparkly grin broke over him. He pushed the engineer's gun aside. "Well, dammit lad, the last time I saw your face you had cheeks like a girl. Now you look like an old convict." He reached a hand down to me. "Come on up here. You remember Rufus Baskinridge?"

It took a minute, but I sure did. 'Course, the Rufus Baskinridge I remembered didn't look like no duke. The Rufus Baskinridge I remembered was an unrespectable rascal who'd run a way station along the trail outside Ft. Wallace, and who'd turned a profit trading liquor and guns to the Indians. The army run him off and that was the last we'd heard of him.

Now Baskinridge helped me and Noah and Bill get settled aboard, with the horses and the mule back in one of the stock cars. Pretty soon all of us were chugging westward. This was my first train ride and I surely picked the right train. Baskinridge had his own private palace car. Here was a feller who like as not used to drink from a horse trough, and now he sat there sipping Scotch whiskey from a crystal glass. He hoisted himself up and struck a pose by the window, resting his hand on the head of this statue of a naked gal carrying a basket of grapes.

He said, "Yes, the West is chock-full of opportunities for the man with ambition. I am humble proof of that. The frontier, gentlemen—the frontier is the American dream brought alive. That's why you found me in the cab of this locomotive. It's my habit to ride up there and watch this vast new land unfold, so full of unlimited promise—by which, of course, I mean the promise of making money."

He puffed at his cigar and continued, "I take it you gentlemen are seeking your fortunes in Colorado?"

I calculated that about half the truth would suffice. "Yessir," I said. "We've heard there's new country openin' up in the northwest part of the state. Hear talk of new gold. Silver, too."

His eyes kind of lit up at that. "I'll let you boys in on something. The rumors are true." Then he straightened up and let fly. "There's gold to be found out there. Lots of it. It'll take grit. It'll take determination. But it's there to be found . . . if you'll spend the sweat and the blood to find it."

Bill said, "By God, sir, I like the sound of that."

There was a knock at the door and the doctor come in. He set up over on the couch and cut the sleeve away from Noah's arm and sent out for a pan of hot water. Noah grumbled some about there being no need for a damn sawbones. But one look at that elbow and anyone knew different.

The doctor said, "What's your name, cowboy?"

Noah said, "My name is Mr. Bowhunter."

The doctor had a real thin mustache—a city mustache. He wrung out a towel and dabbed at Noah's wound.

"Well, Mr. Bowhunter, I'm afraid you're going to lose this arm. We can amputate right here." He almost seemed cheerful about it.

With his good hand Noah wiped his mouth. "There ain't no one-armed cowhands, Doc."

The doctor had that way doctors have, like it's the Almighty come down to talk to you. He said, "The humerus has been shattered just above the elbow. I cannot set bits and pieces of bone. Judging by the inflammation, there is continuing aggravation to the surrounding tissue, and incipient infection."

Noah said, "You sayin' it won't just heal up of its ownself?"

"Might. But even if it does, it will be useless to you from here down." He gave the break just a little poke. "We can expect that after a while it will become infected or even gangrenous. Soon thereafter, you will die."

Noah said, "Is it gangrenous now?"

"No."

"Then I'll just wait on it, I reckon. 'Druther have my arm all in a piece, if I had the choice."

The doctor shrugged his shoulders like it was all of small account to him. He cleaned up the wound, stitched the flesh together with a needle and thread while Noah gritted his teeth. Then the doctor wrapped the elbow lickety-split and rigged a sling around it.

"I wish you the very best, sir," he said. He closed his satchel, collected a fee of four bits, and left the car.

Noah pondered some and said, "Seemed disappointed."

Baskinridge raised his glass to Noah and said, "This one's to you, sir. You've got sand."

Sand or no, I could tell Noah was feeling on the gloomy side. I was, too. Whilst we ate supper, I listened with only half an ear to Baskinridge going on about all the gold we were bound to find in northwest Colorado. Bill was hooked but good.

He said, "But what about the Indians? I heard tell it's Ute country up there."

"It is, at present," said Baskinridge. "The fact is that the whole western part of the state was reserved under the Brunot treaty to the Ute nation . . ." The old boy flicked the ash from his cigar. ". . . Strictly temporary."

Nunan asked what made him say that.

"Because the governor and other forward-looking citizens in the state are determined to rid Colorado of the problem."

I said, "It's a treaty, ain't it?"

"The treaty, son, is irrelevant. We're not going to hold up the march of civilization for the sake of a couple of thousand savages. The Utes must go."

Well, I was thinking, I reckon it's time for Tory Bowhunter to go, too. I got up and thanked old Baskinridge for his hospitality, and he told us we could ride to Denver on his ticket. Bill stayed behind for more speeches about unlimited promise and all that. Me and Noah got out of there and found ourselves a couple of seats in the next car.

The sun was going down and Noah settled in to sleep. Baskinridge had given him one of his fancy silk shirts to replace the one the doctor'd ripped open. He looked right dapper. Well, I thought, at least you got something out of this, Uncle.

I stared out the window and after a time the train stopped for water. I got down and walked back alongside the tracks to the stock car and checked up on Temper and the other animals. I stroked Temper's neck. All the while I was vexed with the thought of Pa alone out there with the Utes.

CHAPTER 4

COME nine o'clock the next evening, we were back in Baskinridge's palace car. Two other fellers was in there with us. Baskinridge called them friends and business associates—Wood Gettys being the tall gray-haired one and John Burnham Antley being the runty one who was drunk.

This Gettys looked to be fifty, or maybe younger but weathered. Plain craggy features, smile lines around the eyes. His hands were big and calloused, with dirt in the pores. He was built rangy but there was breadth to his shoulders, and though he had a little stoop in his walk I got the notion he could whip any two of us. He wore black broadcloth. I took it this Gettys had to be a big auger to move in these circles, but he looked for all the world like a common working man whose wife had made him dress up for church. Except, that is, for the Colt he wore.

As for the short one, we come to find out that this here John Burnham Antley was the son of Jacob Antley, who some years previous had put the Kansas-Pacific Railroad together and got rich doing it. The son was a homely man. He had pop eyes, a pouty sort of mouth, and a weak chin, so that he looked like a kind of fish. Good whiskey smelled no better on his breath than the cheap stuff would on mine.

"Gentlemen," Baskinridge said, "let's play poker."

We settled in around a big round table with a green felt cloth over top. Baskinridge sent for ice. When I saw that bowl of shaved ice—on a train, in August, in Kansas—I knew this here was heady company.

It was a comfy situation there in them leather chairs, with a brass lamp dangling overhead to make a nice warm circle

29

of light to play in. Our host broke out a deck and even the cards had some style to them—each with a thin gold stripe around the edge and a fancy gold RB in the middle. It was a curious feeling to be throwing three months' trail wages in against someone whose monogram was on the cards.

I bought in with my hundred dollars. Noah and Bill each brung a bigger sum into the game as they'd won considerable back in Dodge. Gettys bought in with a thousand. So did Antley. Baskinridge didn't have need to buy chips, as the whole bank belonged to him anyway. He just fetched out a few stacks and lined them up on the felt.

Five-card stud was the game. Baskinridge dealt and Bill won the first hand. Bill got the next deal and won again with eights over fours. One of the fours was his hole card and Antley stayed with him through two raises and lost with a pair of kings.

Bill raked in the pot with both hands. He said, "Someday they're gonna write a book about the way I play poker. They'll call it 'The Legend of Bill Nunan.' "

Antley swore.

Bill's eyebrow went up. He said, "I'll send you a copy."

Noah said, "Best just to play cards, Bill."

Antley's eyes got narrow and mean. He called for a new deck. I had me a more serious problem. We'd played only two hands and half my stake was gone. Two more to match and I'd be busted. I might have stopped right there—but that ain't why you play poker. Under dire circumstances such as these, there weren't much to do but to offer up a tiny prayer for cards.

Prayer might not ordinarily help none, but it rarely hurts. Just to my left Wood Gettys got the deal, and card by card I rode it all the way to a heart flush with the ace on top. Cardplayers tend not to believe that the other feller's flush is gonna pan out. Even four hearts laying there in the open won't convince them—they've got to see your hole card. In my case every man except Gettys paid to see it, and I cashed considerable.

I stacked up the chips and said to Gettys, "I'm beholden to ya."

Gettys chewed his cigar. "Glad to help out, son."

It was my deal now and I made the game draw poker, which was none too bright considering that it stayed that way for a few hands and I lost them all.

Meanwhile Gettys struck up a conversation. He said, "I hear you boys might be headed for Bear River country." I knew him for an old-timer on account of the name had been changed of late to the Yampa River. It was a big river by any name, and Gettys might well have been thinking of any part of northwest Colorado.

"That we are, sir," I said. "We're aimin' to reprovision in Denver and ask around for the quickest way to get out there." I heard Uncle Noah clear his throat, which was by way of advising me that I should watch what I said.

Now I should say a man wouldn't ordinarily cotton to questions on the part of a stranger, but I liked this Gettys feller right off. If he knew the country, he might be worth talking to.

I said, "Been out there yourself?"

He smiled. "Once or twice."

Noah moved the plug around in his mouth. "When was that?"

Gettys said, "Been a year—maybe a hair more. Known that area for quite some time." He pointed his cigar over my way. "Used to trap beaver out around Brown's Hole when I was no older'n this one."

"We heard things might be brewin' out by a town called Tourmaline," I said. "Thought we'd try our luck out thataway."

Gettys laughed. It was a good laugh with nothing in it you'd take offense at. I knew—for at nineteen I could find offense even where none was intended.

He tugged at the corners of his mouth. "Things might be brewing out there, but if they are I've not heard of it. Last I was out thataway, the saloon, the post office, the land office, the dry goods store"—he ticked them off on his fingers—"the barber shop and the whorehouse were all of 'em in the same building. They stabled horses in the back."

Noah laughed. "You're sayin' things weren't exactly booming?"

"Kind of."

Bill said, "Ever meet up with a Wolf Miller?"

Now that there was an interesting question. I looked at Uncle Noah and he looked at me. Neither of us had mentioned Wolf Miller to Bill. That meant he must have been digging around Dodge, asking questions as to what had become of Micah Bowhunter. It might also have meant that, with or without us, he'd been making plans to find Pa.

"You know the Dutchman?" Gettys said.

Bill said, "Heard of him is all."

Gettys eyed his cards, weighing things. He threw two of them down. "Wolf Miller's one of the old mountain breed. Run with Kit Carson and all the rest. Did some trappin'. Scouted some up in Wyoming for the army. Lately I hear he's been supplying game to the Indian Agency at White River. Been among the Utes so long they take him for part of the scenery."

"What you'd call a man of few words," Baskinridge said.

"How's that?" Bill asked.

Gettys said, "He got into a scrape with a couple of Indians some years back and they cut out his tongue."

Bill asked, "Would he know where there's gold?"

Gettys laughed again. "Why sure, son. He's probably waitin' on ya to get out there so you can ask him about it."

The blood rose in Bill's neck. Meantime most of us drew cards and bet again, and Antley laid down three tens and won the hand. Seemed like he'd won two or three in a row.

"I'll tell you what," Gettys said. He reached over and

poured Bill a drink. "The Utes know where the gold is and likely always did. But if you were a Ute you wouldn't let the cat out of the bag, else you'd be overrun with white men even quicker than is already occurring. Now, some old boy like the Dutchman—you've done business with him for years. Somewheres along the line maybe you've given him a clue or two." He poured a shot for himself. " 'Course, maybe you haven't."

This got Bill's curiosity so stirred up, I reckon he forgot to stay mad. "So it could be," he said, "he's out there diggin' right now?"

Gettys smiled sort of sly-like. "Might," he said. "Might not." He had Bill pegged proper, and he was playing with him for fun.

"You hear of any finds out there?" asked Bill.

It was Antley who muttered under his breath, "Jesus."

I felt plumb sorry for Bill. It was piteous. We were in amongst wealthy men, and Bill had his nose pressed up against the glass like a little boy craving candy.

Gettys just studied his cards. I could hear the rails thumping along beneath us. The lamps in the palace car were glinting softly on all the brass and polished mahogany. The smoke from fine cigars hung in the air and smelled good. The whiskey was something special. And Bill was going under. He was disappearing over his head and he didn't even know it.

His voice rose a notch. "I said, you hear of any finds?"

"Mostly, what you hear about," Gettys said, "is Utes."

Suddenly Antley's whiskey glass come banging down on the table, and he shouts, "The Utes must go!"

Thank Godamighty, I thought. At least somebody's taking this here conversation down some other track—even if the one to do it is this ugly little weasel who's just saying what Baskinridge said the night before.

Noah said, "Sounds like somebody's running for office."

"About half the politicians in Colorado are running on

that slogan," said Gettys. He tossed two cards onto the pile. "The Denver papers are full of it."

"I hear tell the Utes been on the prod lately," I said.

Antley swore again. "They sure as hell ain't sittin' around the tepee, whittlin' on sticks."

Noah said, "Heard today they been settin' forest fires everywhere. Any truth in that?"

"It's an unfortunate business," Gettys said. "They got their reservation lands through treaty, and now it's turning out like all the other treaties. So, best they can, they fight back."

Baskinridge leaned forward. "Which is to say they got too much the first time around." What come next was another speech like we'd growed accustomed to, full of stuff like "Civilization, gentlemen, requires room for expansion . . ." "The march of white society to the Pacific cannot be stemmed to accommodate savages . . ." "Those among the red men that cannot be civilized must be eradicated."

When the big wind had passed, he settled back again and blew smoke. "We've faced their savagery before. It's no different this time."

"Anybody get killed so far?" Bill said. Gettys answered that a farmer had been burned out, his wife and child murdered as well. Other than that, just rumors.

Antley said, "Fact is, most ain't lived to tell of it. Raping white women and killing babies is just sport for Utes."

"I think Colonel Chivington said it best," Baskinridge said. "You'll recollect, after the victory at Sand Creek."

The name Chivington hadn't struck much of a chord right off, but there wasn't one of us hadn't heard of what happened at Sand Creek twelve or fifteen years previous. Back then the Sioux and Arapaho had put a scare in the white folks of Denver. The army harried the Indians some and finally offered them a cessation of hostilities if they'd make camp on the Big Bend of Sand Creek. The site was maybe a day's ride northeast of Ft. Lyon, in the southeast part of the state. So the Sioux and the Arapaho and all their squaws and children and dogs and horses settled in. As soon as they let their guard down, the commander of the First and Third Coloradoes, who turned out to be this feller Chivington, charged his men in at daybreak and wiped them out. Four hundred Indians, maybe more, roused from their sleep and massacred.

Following that, Colorado didn't have no Sioux or Arapaho problem.

"The colonel knew how to handle the issue," Baskinridge said. Once again he leaned forward in his chair, like to share a secret with us. "You know, they asked him why he and his troops killed the Indian babes along with their parents."

"And what'd he say?"

"He said nits make lice."

We bet around and Antley won again.

The game come back to five-card stud when I won the biggest hand of the night. The deal was Gettys's and he had to fold on the third card. The rest of us all hung in there till the bitter end, and Gettys dropped me a third king to win it.

So far Rufus Baskinridge was the big loser, tossing chips on the pile like they didn't mean much to him. Which I guess they didn't. Bill played the same way. Them first few hands had gone to Bill's head, till everything he'd won was gone—and some of what he'd brung in with him, too. Now it was Bill that asked for a new deck. Antley, though, even glazed over like he was, kept buying cards and winning hands.

The game grew serious. We were due into Denver by midmorning, and it looked like we might still be playing when we got there. I dealt a hand and nothing much developed, but Antley got it next and dealt himself a ten-high straight to win.

Bill said, "You been winnin' a mite regular."

Antley was slow to pick up on that. Noah was half through with his deal—and that was slow enough, him going through the motions one-handed—when Antley realized Bill had just about called him a cheat.

All Antley could get out was, "Why, you . . ."

"Easy, boys." It was Baskinridge. "I'm sure we would all regret breaking up this friendly recreation over a misunderstanding."

They left it at that. The next pot went to Gettys, and the one after that, too. Bill got the deal. A pair of queens drove his hopes up but I won on the last card. His eyes flared up at me. I reckon Noah saw it because he said, "Boys, let's pack it in."

"We ain't packin' nothing in," Bill said.

"No, no, you hang in there," Antley said, perking up like somebody'd just wakened him from a nap. "Luck's gotta turn." He looked over at Bill and smiled, his eyes like a couple of raw oysters. I'd just as soon picked up my chips right then, but you couldn't ask Bill to back off from this feller. If Bill was amind to stay, so was I.

We anted up and Gettys dealt the cards—the first one face down, the next one up. You heard each one snap on the table.

None of us got much to brag on save for Bill and Antley. Both showed aces, and on the next card Bill got another. Antley got the ten of hearts.

Me and Noah folded. I kinda figured it would boil down to Bill and the little man. And I knew it for a dead certainty when Bill bet his pair of aces, and Antley took a long drag off his cigar and then raised him.

That said something. It said that Antley held the other ace—or else he was a drunken man betting tens against aces—or else he was bluffing. Bill must have thought it was a bluff. He raised him back.

Gettys had already dropped out, and even Baskinridge called it quits on the next go-round when Antley pulled another ten. Now he could have two pair, aces and tens, or he might have three tens. Nunan bought the three of clubs and his aces were still the bet. He tossed in fifty dollars' worth of chips.

Antley raised him again.

Bill pondered on it maybe a frog's hair too long for a man with an ace in the hole. But he saw the little man and raised him back.

Gettys dealt Bill his fifth card. Another three. Two pair showing, aces and threes, with the possibility that we were looking at a full house, aces up. Then Gettys dealt Antley another ten.

That made it three tens showing, and the way Antley let out an itty-bitty squeal like a piglet made, you guess there was another one underneath.

"Three tens are the bet," Gettys said.

You could see Antley's eyes pore over Bill's chips—what was left of them. His tongue flicked out and licked his lips, and he bet exactly what he counted in front of Bill—one hundred eighty dollars. It was pocket change to John Burnham Antley, a man born with money, and who'd likely never put together two hours' work in his life. But to Bill Nunan, one hundred eighty dollars was blood.

Bill pushed in his chips.

Antley wet his lips again and smiled. "Sure hope you find gold in Colorado."

Then he put his fingers around his hole card and very slowly turned it over. A ten would make it four of a kind. An ace would make it a full house, tens over aces. What's more, an ace would be the fourth to show. It would mean there was no way Bill could beat him—unless this deck held five aces.

Antley's hole card was the ace of spades.

That ought to do it, I said to myself, but before the thought was half finished Bill sprung to his feet and shouted, "You cheatin' sonofabitch!" and come up over the table at the little man so's the whole setup overturned and cards and chips and glasses full of whiskey went flying everywhere. Everyone either fell or jumped back from the table, knocking into other pieces of furniture which also come crashing onto the floor. Baskinridge tumbled over backwards and on the way down he grabbed for the whiskey cart and pulled that down along with him.

My first thought was that someone was about to get shot. Bill was swinging every which way and Antley was pushing Bill off him. Suddenly Antley reached inside his belt. Bill was making a move to charge him again but stopped when he saw that Antley had a gun—and Bill didn't.

CHAPTER 5

OUT it come, just a little derringer or somesuch as a woman might carry—but out of the shadows nearby another hand flashed into view, this one with a big Colt revolver in it, and just as Antley jerked the trigger the Colt smashed the derringer from his fingers.

It was fortunate for the old girl with the grapes on her head that she was just a piece of rock, 'cause she took it in the breast. The ricochet shattered the window alongside her, and suddenly we could hear the clatter of the rails and the wind rushing in.

It was Wood Gettys that knocked the gun from Antley's hand. He brung the Colt back up and struck him smartly alongside the temple. The little man hadn't far to drop, but he hit the carpet with a good substantial thud. Gettys reached up with his free hand and steadied the lamp.

He turned to Bill. "Now tell me, son, what's this all about?"

Bill was still hot. "That cheatin' sonofabitch!"

Gettys laid the weight of his eyes on Bill—the way you might snare the eye of a horse you're trying to break, and then just by talking real quiet-like you let him know who's in charge.

"You come nigh on to gettin' someone shot over this," Gettys said. "I reckon you ought to make good on what you claim."

"There was three aces showing on the table and I held the other," Nunan said. "The little sonofabitch found himself another ace."

Now Gettys said, "No offense, son, but we never did see your hole card."

I spoke up. "If he says it was an ace, he ain't lyin'."

Bill held up his hand to me. "That's all right," he said. He run his fingers back through his hair. "I'm truly sorry, Mr. Gettys. It's just I go loco when I'm cheated."

It seemed the only way to settle this was to count up the cards, so we started combing through the wreckage—and by God if in ten minutes we didn't locate five aces, each with that gold RB on the back.

"Why, that little bastard," Baskinridge said. The little bastard himself lay there on the rug.

"I'm awfully sorry to sully up your car, sir," Bill said, all calmed down now. "I hope I can make good for it."

"Wouldn't hear of it, son," Baskinridge said. "None of us likes injustice. We'll settle up your fair share of the chips and make certain you leave with more than what you brought in. As your host I take responsibility for Mr. Antley's indiscretion." He dropped his gaze down onto the little man. "When he wakens I'm gonna knock him out myself."

Through all this I hadn't heard much out of Noah. When I looked around I found him kind of slumped in one of Baskinridge's big cushiony chairs.

"What's happened?" I said.

The sweat stood out on his forehead. "Fell on my arm."

Seemed like a fit time to wrap things up for the night. We bid Baskinridge good night—all of us but Bill, who was hot to split up the chips with the old boy, and Antley, who was still in repose. I told Baskinridge just to let Bill bring by our share of the money. I got Noah out of there and settled him in as best I could. I needed some rest myself but what I wanted first was a smoke.

I tarried outside between the cars, and for the first time that night things grew peaceful inside me. There were many more stars overhead than a man could count—'cept when the tracks took a turn and the white plume of the engine blowed by overhead—and away in the darkness I could see a lantern in the window of some nester who'd grown prosperous enough to have a window, and it was cool out there and good to be alone and rolling a smoke.

Before I could light up I had company.

"Pleasant night," Gettys said.

He struck a match and cupped those big hands of his round it for me to take a light. For himself he fired up a long thin cigar and leaned back against the gate.

I said, "I want to say thanks to you for saving my friend's life."

He brushed it aside. "Your friend takes chances."

It was true, of course, but him pointing it out like that kinda threw me. I said, "Well, that's just Bill."

"And that's just my observation, son. But I've seen men like him before, and what I'm sayin' is that it might pay you to stay loose around him. You're uncle knows what I mean."

I said, "How's that?"

"You ask him."

We rumbled along there for a spell. I got to inquiring what he did and he told me about himself. He was born to a farming family in the Western Reserve—good Presbyterian stock but hard on the mavericks, and to hear him tell it that's what he was. One night at a dance he fought a man and killed him—"Nothing so uncommon where you come from," he said, "but serious business among settled folk." Then he was sent off to join the army so's matters could cool down. Wasn't long before he was at Buena Vista fighting under Zachary Taylor. There he picked up a knowledge of explosives—"Just took to it natural, I reckon." He spent a fair amount of time pulverizing Mexicans. When he got back to Ohio the old homestead seemed a mite dull by comparison, and since folks didn't seem to want him around that bad anyhow, he left for the West. That was 1848.

He was among them that opened the country. He hunted in Colorado and Wyoming, trapped beaver with Bridger and Sublette and the rest of their ilk, and run west to California when gold turned up at John Sutter's mill. Gettys never found none himself. But he happened upon plenty of folks who whilst they looked needed mountains blowed open, and who didn't want to run the risks themselves. He made a good living at it.

Twenty years later he'd built several businesses—mining, stockyards, freight hauling, machine works. "Thing is," he said, "I still like to blow things up. Don't know why. Crave excitement, I guess."

Speaking this way, a wistful kind of sound come into Gettys's voice, like fellers get out on the trail when they talk about women. I laughed. Gettys heard it and mulled it over, and he laughed, too.

I decided to trust this man—though I reckon it ain't really a thing you decide. You just come to feel it. It might be something in his words, or in his deeds, or just in the lines of his face. I reached inside my vest and fetched out Pa's letter.

He held it up by the lantern and squinted at it. "Interesting postmark."

I give him a while to decipher Pa's hand. "What do you think?"

The whistle blowed and he had to shout for the noise. "Don't know. Could be gold. Silver, maybe."

Whichever it was, Pa'd written to me two months previous and I was still in Kansas. I told Gettys how the letter had been waiting for me at the end of the cattle drive, and how I'd learned of Wolf Miller from Sarie Clement, and how my uncle and me had set out for Colorado and run into Comanches, and how Bill had showed up just in time to save my life.

I said to Gettys, "All this, and I ain't halfway to Tourmaline."

Gettys said, "I'll get you there." He explained that he'd bid low on a contract to haul annuity goods to the Ute Indian Agency on White River. It was the same place he'd said Wolf Miller was selling game, in a valley called Powell Park, on the southern edge of the Danforth Hills and some seventy or eighty miles to the southwest of Steamboat Springs.

He said, "What do you know about bullwhackin'?"

I thought hard about lying but I just shook my head.

"Good," he said. "Then I won't have to pay you wages. You just tag along with the bull train and help out if they need it. Your uncle can loaf in one of the wagons and rest his arm. It'll be a good-sized outfit—ten wagons, thirty-three oxen. Mostly seed wheat, flour, bobwire, a couple of cook stoves. Two hundred pairs of shoes for the Utes. The outfit'll pull out of Denver later today—leastways they'd better, as I'm payin' them. You ought to make the Gore Pass in less than two weeks. Once you're through there, you split off from 'em and head north. After that it's a three-day ride to Tourmaline. I'll draw you a map."

I thought of one more thing. "You said me and my uncle were welcome, sir. What about Bill?"

Gettys laughed again. "Seems you're set on bringing your own explosives."

It was easy to laugh with him. "That I am, sir."

He nodded. "Then it's all right with me."

By now the stars were fading, and I'd rolled myself considerable more than the one smoke I'd intended. Missing a night's sleep is nothing when you're used to trailin' steers. And tarrying longer was right pleasurous, listening to Gettys's stories and the bumping of the rails. He'd roamed from Mexico to the British Possessions and all points in between, been all over Europe and into places I'd never heard of.

"Let me tell you about someone you're gonna meet," he said. "A gent from my Ohio days, name of Nathan Meeker. When I first knew him he was in the dry-goods business. A real fancy thinker, though. A socialist. Left town to join a utopian community in Euclid called Trumbull Phalanx. After that he took up newspapering in New York City. Then he founded Greeley, Colorado. Went bankrupt after that. I haven't seen him in thirty years, but I've read about him from time to time."

I weren't sure of one or two of the words Gettys used.

More than that, I weren't sure of what any of this had to do with me. So I asked.

Gettys said, "You're heading for the Ute Indian Agency at White River, right?"

I nodded.

"Nathan Meeker is the Indian Agent. Say hello to him for me."

A couple of miles outside Denver, we come up onto a siding by the stockyards. Whilst they unloaded the beef for Denver, we got the five horses and the mule down off there. Once we'd clumb off the ramp and onto steady ground, Temper let me know just how he felt about being locked up in the dark for two days with a bunch of cows. He made it a special experience for me just to slap the saddle on his back. On my third try I told him he'd be saddled or he'd be horsemeat. Once he could tell that I was sorely vexed with him, he was satisfied and let me throw it on him.

Things were right busy by the siding, whole herds of people bustling around in the plaza to meet the train, wagons rolling in to haul off the freight, hooves and wagon wheels raising dust and commotion everywhere and the noise of cattle bawling down the planks into the stock pens and buckboards clattering and folks hallooing to one another.

"This is just a taste of Denver, son," Baskinridge said. He had to shout for me to hear. "Wait till you're in the city proper."

I was feeling kindly toward Baskinridge. He'd settled up all the finances from the poker game and Bill had come by with four hundred dollars for me and even more for Noah. As for Bill, instead of losing all he had, he'd come out ahead. Noah had looked at Bill kinda slaunchwise and said, "Tough way to make a living."

I got aholt of Gettys over by where he was watching the stock unload, and asked him just where to go to tie up with his freighters. He said they'd be off in the direction of

Central City, and if we cared to tarry with him in Denver we could catch up with them anytime in the next couple of days.

He said, "Rufus and me will be dining with the governor tonight. You boys might like to join us."

I thought hard on that one. "That's awful kind of you, Wood, but I been talkin' it over with Noah and Bill. They're eager to be going—as I am."

"Well, you'll be missed," he said. "How's that uncle of yours?"

"He told me that if I asked him about his arm one more time, he'd break mine."

Gettys grinned. "That man's all right."

Gettys was all right, too. I gave him the Indian pony as a gift. He took the reins in hand and just kinda nodded—but in his look I could see it meant considerable.

He had a letter already writ out so's we could show it to his freight crew. I tucked that in with the map he'd drawn me, and after a few more pleasantries I was set to ride.

"One more thing, son." Gettys's eyes took hold of mine, like this was just between us two. "Your friend Bill didn't have no ace in the hole."

"How's that?"

"It was the three of hearts."

I just stared.

"When we were all down on the floor searching for aces? He slipped one out of his vest. I reckon he secreted it away when we changed decks."

I said, "You saw this?"

"I did."

"But you could of . . ."

"Yes, I could have shot him right there. But if I'd have called him on it, you would've stood by him, wouldn't you?"

"Yes, if I hadn't seen it myself."

He smiled. "I didn't want me and you to tangle, not for his likes. No pleasure in that."

I felt plumb sick. I said, "No, sir."

"It's all right, son. A man has to know who he's riding with." His eyes held steady with mine. "Your friend talks too much. He takes chances. And he cares too much for money."

I straightened my back in the saddle and reached out to shake his hand. "Thank you, sir."

"You look me up when this is over."

"That I will."

I reined over toward Noah and Bill. I had much to chew on. I saw Bill some ways off and I just wished I didn't like him. Then I thought of something.

I brung Temper back around. "Hey, Wood," I said. "Bill's hole card—the three of hearts? How would you know that?"

"Tory boy," he begun, and that sly smile commenced to work its way across his lips. "I dealt the cards."

Part 2

By Way of White River

CHAPTER 6

WE were twelve days with that bull train, rolling easy out of Denver and westward into the foothills—but it weren't so easy thereafter. Slow and treacherous up through canyon country towards Central City, and slower still on that snaky trail to Idaho Springs they call Omigod Road. And then northward to the high mountains, and up over Berthoud's Pass. It's a good thing that oxen are too dumb to be afraid of heights, and of shelf rock that gives way underneath you, and of rocks and snow that can tumble down onto you. But I reckon the brutes also miss something by being too dumb to know beauty when they see it. For we crossed the Divide at something more than eleven thousand feet, where the snow has never melted and the air is like good whiskey, sharp and smooth at once. And what the eyes beheld passed directly into a man's heart, and you knew that crazy feeling, like you sometimes know with a horse or a pretty woman, of coming to love something that can kill you without hardly trying.

We drove further to the northward up toward Grand Lake, where you might stretch out your hand and splay your fingers, and it would seem like each finger touched the crest of a different mountain. From there, westward through Middle Park, sleeping in meadows where you wakened to the hum of bees in the yellow clover. The streams ran low in these summer days, but their channels cut deep. It was generous country. You knew it would fill up one day, and even afterwards folks would keep pressing back the frontier until all the land—even the reservation lands that lay to the west—were tamed and brought under the plow.

We rolled onto the Gore Pass-Middle Park Road, paid the

toll, and somehow kept the wheels on the wagons long enough to get over. On the yon side of the Gore Range, we thanked the boys and split off from them. I got out the little map that Gettys drew up and we wended northward up the Yampa River into Steamboat Springs. Past that Uncle Noah, Bill, and I followed Elk Creek toward Hahn's Peak and climbed into the mountains in the direction of North Park, following the old Indian trails that Gettys had mapped for us. We were into evergreen country. The trails didn't lack for signs of being used. Lately, too.

Few white men had gotten into these parts—just them, I reckon, as had got a whiff of the news that there might be an ounce or two of dust left if a feller was amind to make the journey. It was rough going, but it was good to see Noah handling it, his arm still in the sling but mending. We come round a turn in the trail—stepping careful through the slide rock and limber pine—and below the ridge there was half a mile's worth of alpine valley. We picked our way down to it. Then we stared—stared long and hard.

Bill said, "Welcome to Tourmaline."

Noah said, "What's left of it."

What was left of it weren't much. Not a whole lot remained but the burned-out shell of that building Gettys had bespoken—the one that was part saloon and post office and whore-house and whatnot. He'd been right—there hadn't been much more to Tourmaline. But that was considerable more than what was left.

The damage hadn't been done more than a month or two previous because the grass had not come back. I thought of where Pa might be in all this—and then other thoughts come tumbling in over one another. I could hear myself speak, like it was someone else talking far off. I said, "The Utes must go."

Noah said, "Looks to me, Tory boy, like they already come and went."

We dismounted and tied the horses. Me and my uncle

poked around the ashes and turned up the bones that the buzzards and magpies had left behind. The town of Tourmaline had made a good hot fire. There weren't much left but scraps of things.

Noah said, "You know, there's somethin' curious in this."

He took a charred stick in his good hand and used it to turn something up out of the ashes. I ain't eager to relate what it was, but some half-burnt satin cloth still clung to it.

He said, "An Indian would call this wasteful."

I reckoned that was true. They didn't kill a woman right off. Better to take her back to the lodge. Men captured weren't much worth saving except to torture. But a woman— Indians usually took her, would trade her off for dogs or horses, or even make a squaw of her. Yet here in Tourmaline they'd killed the women right along with the men.

Just then, down on my haunches, staring at what the fire and the birds had left of a woman, if I'd have heard a ki-yi come down out of the hills and seen the Utes riding down on us in a pack it would not have surprised me a'tall. But we didn't hear a thing. Just wind, and stillness.

We scouted up the trail a ways. Bill rode point. None of us knew the country, but from what we'd seen of it there must be hundreds of canyons and draws where Pa might be hid away. We might search from one canyon to the next right on into winter.

We made camp where the trail ducked in against the rocky face of the mountain. The rocks overhung us for cover at our back. There was plenty of brush for the stock to browse through, and a cold spring flowed from a crevasse in the rocks. Fifteen yards or so before us the shelf fell away into the valley, so's no one could approach from that direction. Nonetheless we kept the fire low.

Bill was clearly vexed. "Seems like we come a powerful distance to inquire after your pa," he said, "and they didn't leave us nobody to inquire with."

I said, "What do you reckon we ought to do?"

He spat some coffee into the fire. It sizzled. "Fan out," he said. "We'll just comb these hills till we find the old boy."

" 'Fraid not," I said. "We ain't gonna find Pa on our own, not in this country."

"You tellin' me we just up and quit?" Nunan said. "Now that we can practically smell it? Tory boy, we come too damn far not to . . ."

"Not to cash in?" Noah said.

Bill straightened up. "To find his pa. Your brother."

Noah laughed.

I said, "Look, Bill. Sarie told me Pa'd left Dodge with Wolf Miller. That's about all we got left to go on. Gettys told us Wolf Miller's workin' for the agency at White River."

"So?"

"So's we head over there."

His jaw dropped open. "That's a hundred miles off."

"Maybe so."

Bill turned to Noah. "How's this set with you, pardner?"

"This here is Tory's show. It's his pa."

You could almost hear the steam leak out of Bill. "You boys are lettin' the big one get away."

There weren't much for me and Noah to say. Bill sputtered some but when it sunk in that he wasn't getting anywhere the fight petered out and he spat another mouthful of coffee into the fire.

This time the fire exploded.

Sparks and cinders burst up at us and rained onto the grass. Funny how a notion'll come to you, but my first thought was that that must have been right strong coffee. But I realized it was gunfire that done it, and now the second shot whanged off the rock behind us. We hit the ground and kicked dirt up over the fire to douse the light and another shot clipped the leaves overhead.

"What have you got?" Bill whispered.

"I'm all right. Noah?"

"One gun across the way. No, two. Close by each other."

A rifle flashed. Lead sang through the leaves again. Noah made it a hundred fifty yards distant. Then another round, this one lower into the face of the mountain at our back. We heard the spray of splintered rock falling through the leaves—then silence.

Bill said, "How do you reckon they can see us?"

"I ain't sure they can," Noah said. "They're blastin' all over creation."

I said, "I'm gonna crawl out there a ways and see what we're up against."

"No, you ain't," Noah said. "You're gonna stay put while we wait it out."

We were pinned there—pure and simple—and so we might have stayed but worse luck took over. One of the embers from out of the campfire suddenly flickered to life amongst the brush, and when it did the flames roared up. Temper and the other horses begun to stamp and squawl, and above the whole ruckus we could hear the mule hee-haw. Another shot boomed out from yonder across the valley and that shelf we'd camped on was lit up as bright as the stage at the Lady Gay. The three of us broke for the horses, but I'd already took my boots off for the night and had to find them, and then there was saddles to throw up on the animals—and Noah wasn't going to handle that too quick what with one good arm. The horses wouldn't stand still to be saddled in the midst of a fire. I gave up trying and drug my saddle with one hand while I yanked Temper and the blue roan along with the other. I kept them close to the face of the wall so's to follow the trail around and out of sight of the Indians. Bill did the same with his horse and the mule. I looked over my shoulder for Noah and caught a glimpse of him struggling with the sorrell, yelling "Whoa!" and straining at the reins with his good arm till the beast reared back on his hind legs and crushed Noah up against the rocks.

You could hear Noah cry out even over the roar of the fire. I let go the reins and slapped Temper on the rump and he

took off, and I heaved my saddle aside and run back to
Noah. The sorrel charged past me, his eyes wide with fear. I
got down by Noah and looked him over. He'd got his forehead bashed against the wall and the blood was still coming.
I thought, God, he's gonna die, but soon I took the blood for
a good sign 'cause his heart must still be pumping. I couldn't
tell what else was busted up, but I knew we had trouble
a'plenty—Noah was unconscious, fire was spreading through
the brush, and lead was still flying. Then around the wall
comes Bill Nunan, and he's got his Winchester with him.

I had me the task of pulling Noah out of there, and I
needed some cover to do it. Bill took one look at me and my
uncle and he grinned like a kid with a new pony. He turned
to where the shots were coming from, caught sight of a
muzzle flash across the valley, and begun to fire back.

Once is all you get to see a thing such as that—this big
cowboy raring back on his heels, his face lit up by flames
against the smoke and the black of the night, the butt of his
Winchester down by his hip and him blasting away into the
dark like the Lord's right hand. It was something to behold.
I grabbed Uncle Noah under the arms and drug him round
the bend in the wall. Bill's horse and the mule were already
tied to a tree limb. Temper stood there handy and I guessed
we'd find the blue roan and the sorrel not too far distant. I
laid Noah down as easy as I could.

In a minute Bill was with us. I left Noah with him and ran
back around the wall and snatched my saddle out of the fire
and by then I was about ready to stop and catch my breath.

Bill's eyes were bright with excitement, like a boy. I said,
"You should of done your shooting from behind a tree."

He said, "Tory boy, ain't no fun from back of no tree." He
went to round up the horses.

I dabbed at Noah's forehead and wrapped it with my
bandanna. He come around but moaned so that I knew
something more was paining him.

"The arm," he said. The pain made him short of breath. "Tory, it's that goddamned arm."

I looked down at it, the elbow all bloody again right through the sling, and my heart sank.

"Can you ride, Uncle?"

"It's that goddamned arm."

I had to shout at him. "We got to ride, Noah. We still got us Indian problems."

I wasn't certain we did, but this was surely no place to tarry. When Bill got there with the other horses, I stood up and saddled Temper and the blue roan. Then I hoisted Noah onto Temper's back and mounted the roan myself. Through the darkness, I led us out of there.

We kept moving till first light. We made camp just long enough to catnap, and then afterwards me and Bill rigged up a travois for Noah out of birch branches, Indian style. We hung as best we could to level ground, but mostly what we did was pick our way through the gullies and canyons and search out gaps among the hills. The mule drug the travois, and when the mule tired we made use of the roan. When we come onto a creek, Bill and me would unhitch the travois and carry it ourselves.

What we couldn't do much of was rest. It took us three days to reach Hayden—just halfway to White River. Back of the saloon they had what passed for a boardinghouse and I bought Noah a bed for the night. There was no doctor, nor was there a man among the dozen or so that made up that town who knew what to do with a shattered arm. I wondered if we should just hang fire awhile before we pushed on. Maybe if we gave Noah some time, he'd get his strength back. But in the room that night, by the light of a low kerosene flame, I cut away the sleeve of that silk shirt Baskinridge give him and washed his elbow—it leaked with something greenish and foul-smelling—and as I did, I wondered just how much time we had.

Before the sun rose we began to work our way southward again. Toward dusk we made camp by a lake as blue as anything I'd ever seen, with fir-covered hills swooping up around it on three sides, and deer so thick you'd catch glimpses of them browsing amongst the trees. But for all the loveliness of the place there was no pleasure in it, for when I looked upon the mountains, all I thought of was more hard travel.

In the night a fever come upon Noah, and he began to talk in his sleep like he thought he was elsewhere. I laid his blanket on him and atop that my yellow slicker, but his teeth kept rattlin'. My watch come first but even when Bill took over from me I laid awake with my uncle.

The next day passed, and the dark come on and still another morning. I rode alongside the travois and sometimes we stopped so's I could mop the sweat from off Noah's forehead or give him something for his thirst. It was rugged going, and with him grown so quiet, sleeping that restless, talking sleep, there was no telling how bad off he was. All I knew was the pale look of him and the way his eyes didn't seem to see, and the way his clothes were soaking wet and the words that he spoke didn't make no sense. One time he called me Micah.

It weighed on me that we might reach White River and not find a trace of Wolf Miller, or even a doctor that might tend to Noah. We'd have come this distance for nothing.

We topped a rise just then and a valley lay before us. A mile distant a river glittered like a silver ribbon, bordered by willows and box elder. On the yon side, three or four miles distant to the southward, the hills bulked up big and brown like so many sacks of grain.

Closer in, on the near side and downstream a quarter-mile or so, we saw fence posts.

"Noah," I said, "this is gonna be all right."

We worked our way down the slope, careful and slow on Noah's account, and crossed through patches of clover and rabbit brush to the river. In the shade thereabouts we watered the animals. Then we followed the river downstream. It took a turn, and half a dozen buildings came in sight—all of them laid out neat as a pin, one a big frame building with two stories and an awning over the porch. In the street before the livery barn, the wagons of Gettys's bull train stood empty. On the outskirts a mile distant, fifty, maybe sixty tepees—Indians moving among them, and hundreds of grazing ponies. Farther on, the wilderness again—steep, rocky hills dotted with sagebrush as far as a man's sight would carry.

We come onto four fellers belly-deep in a trench. Some time previous they'd started digging by the riverbank. Now they had a good three hundred yards of ditch in their wake. They were all working hard on a sweat and kept at it even as we drew up. Bill caught the attention of the one with the big shoulders—a red-haired feller with his shirt off and eyes that kind of crisscrossed on you.

Bill said, "What are you all up to, boy?"

The feller took off his hat and wiped the back of his forearm across his brow. He spat tobacco juice and smiled real broad.

"Well, sir. This here's the White River Indian Agency. We're irrigatin'."

CHAPTER 7

THIS feller went by the name of Shadrach Price. Him and another farmboy, name of Hickett, took aholt of the travois as I unhitched it and they carried Noah up the slope to the agency. They wrassled him in through the side door of the big agency house and laid him on a long plank table in the kitchen.

There was a pair of Utes sitting at the table gnawing on chicken bones. Shadrach and Hickett laid Noah right down in the middle of things but them Utes hardly looked up. They'd have gone on eating right around him if the boys hadn't told them to scat. Shadrach turned to this little Indian girl who'd been talking with them and told her to go get some help.

Noah called out something about blizzards. It might have been buzzards, we couldn't hardly tell. He was thrashing about on the table, the sweat rolling off him and his tongue lolling out.

The Indian girl came back with a tall man. He had a head full of gray hair and his eyes were blue as a robin's eggs. He was followed by a girl and a couple more boys about the age of Shadrach and Hickett.

"Mr. Meeker," Shadrach says. "These here fellers come in just now and . . ."

"So I heard, Shadrach. Let me see the man's injury."

Bill reached down and pulled aside the blanket. Meeker changed color, from pink to pale green. All he could choke out was, "This man needs help!"

"I knew that," I said.

Someone else spoke up. It was the girl who'd come in with

him. She had blue eyes just like his, and she was as pretty and yellow-haired a thing as I ever seen.

"Jane," she said to the Indian girl. "Run over to the blacksmith and have him heat up a flat piece of iron. Get it red-hot. Leave enough to wrap some cloth around for a handle. Tell him to bring it here the moment it's ready."

"Yes, Miss Josie," she said and lit out of there.

By now Meeker was over by the wall where they'd leaned the travois. His knees weren't holding real good. Josie said, "Hickett, take my father out for some air."

Bill said, "I'll do it."

"Shadrach," Josie said. "Bring me some sheets from upstairs." She sent one of the other boys out to draw water and heat it up on the stove. She sent Hickett to fetch a saw. Then she turned my way.

"Is this man your friend?"

I thought, by God, this here's just a little girl. "What are you gonna do to my uncle?"

By way of an answer, all she did was to draw my gaze down to Noah's arm. It was an ugly thing, swole up to twice what it should have been. Where the wound was, the skin was tight and shiny, purple in color. It leaked pus. Yellow streaks run back from there into Noah's armpit.

The girl's eyes looked up into mine, and they spoke plenty. They said we had this here job to do, and it was hers and mine to do it.

"I'm with you," I said.

Those blue eyes smiled. "What's his name?" she asked.

I told her his name and mine, and she put her hand on Noah's brow and stroked it. Josie went over by the wall directly and got down a metal box and laid it by Noah's head. She unbuckled the straps and fetched out a little brown bottle and uncorked it.

"Mr. Bowhunter, I'm going to give you something now so you won't feel so much pain." She poured out a spoonful of red liquid, like a syrup, and put it to his lips. "That's tincture of opium," she said to me. "Mostly it's used to quiet the bowel."

It quieted Noah considerable. His teeth stopped chattering so much, and he trembled less so's it was easier to hold him still. His eyes growed soft.

Josie felt his wrist. "That's good," she said. "Get the knife."

Jane had come back in. She brung Josie the knife, the blade broad and shining. It was just a regular butcher knife, about as long as Josie's forearm.

The blacksmith showed up with the hot iron.

Josie said, "Lay it in the stove. And stay handy."

We were a crowded bunch in that little kitchen. The light come in through one small window and the open door, and the room had growed hot and smelled ripe with men's sweat and the corruption in Noah's wound. Josie placed me up by his shoulder, looking down the length of the bad arm. She was at his elbow. She tied a length of clothesline high up on the arm, and to keep the bleeding down she twisted the line tight with a piece of kindling. She poured whiskey into a swatch of linen and washed the skin. Then she slipped a smaller chunk of wood between Noah's teeth.

She said, "Ready?"

I gripped Noah's shoulder. His eyes come up to mine.

I recollected a day long previous to this. Me and Noah were duck hunting down by the Gulf. I had a bird dog back then I called Blue Johnny. He was more fire than smarts, this one was, and this morning he's high-tailin' it over the marsh and jumps a cypress log at full bore. He doesn't see there's this broken branch jutting out from the log and it gores him clean through. When I catch up with him, he's skewered there on the jagged end, panting hard, his tongue hanging out and his eyes staring up about as still as death. He's waiting to see how I'm gonna get him out of this.

I looked in Noah's eyes and what I recalled was the look Blue Johnny had. *Well, by God,* I thought, *I ain't losing this uncle of mine, so let 'er rip.* And just then Josie leaned into the blade and cleaved down through the muscle of Noah's arm. His body come near to jumping off the table—someone shouted, "Hold him down, Goddamn it!"—and quickly Josie turned the knife upside down and drew it up through the soft underside.

It was a frightful moan come out of Noah. But then his eyes turned up into his head and he was out.

Josie said, "Tory, pull the flesh back." I pressed my fingertips into the arm just above the cut and pulled back the meat till the bone showed. Then Josie had the blade of the saw down in there and she drove the teeth into it, then back, and into it and back again, and again, and before too long the arm thudded onto the floor and she shouted, "The iron!" and the blacksmith put it in her hand.

She said to me, "Hold it steady." I grasped the stump with my hands. I just about strangled the thing, I squoze so hard to stop the blood. Then she brung the glowing part of the iron up against it. It sizzled, the way a steak sizzles when you drop it on the griddle. The smoke come up so sharp into my face that it stung my eyes.

I eased my grip and I laid the stump down as gentle as I could. There was no rubbing my eyes as my hands were all bloodied. Then Josie dipped a clean swatch of linen in the water and washed the sting out of my vision. I saw her clear—her face glistening, staring back at me, all filled with relief and pride—and though other folks had lent a hand, it felt like it was me and Josie Meeker that had come through the fire.

I said, "Ma'am, you're a piece of work."

We got Noah into a bed upstairs. The room they gave us was tiny but a comfy place, wallpapered with little blue flowers. Out one window I could see the Indian lodges off to the westward. The other window looked over the street. It was called Josie's Lane, on account it was her father who laid out this here agency and got to name all the streets himself.

When the opium wore off, Noah commenced to trembling again, and the fever took aholt of him as strong as ever. But Josie was there to nurse him. She dressed the stump of his arm in wet linen and sponged the sweat from off his body, and when he lay still enough to take a sip of beef tea she got that into him—and while I couldn't do much for him myself, I had faith that Josie could.

She had some help from her ma, Arvilla Delight Meeker, a woman just as little as Josie was but with more tallow on her. I was thankful that Josie favored her pa, for Arvilla very much resembled a toad or somesuch homely creature.

I tried to picture what Arvilla had looked like at Josie's age. She was kindly dispositioned, and though she smiled about as often as a rock, her goodness shown clear. She came up the stairs with half a roasted chicken and a glass of milk, just so's I could eat and not have to quit Noah's side. When she heard we hadn't made camp the previous night on Noah's account, she made me pull off my boots and take some rest in the bed next to his. She knew a man's needs about as well as any woman I'd come across.

I guess she knew her husband's needs as well, for she told me she'd been with him in the days when he'd sold dry goods in Ohio, and when he tied up with that commune called Trumbull Phalanx, and then through the years of scraping to make a name for himself in the newspaper business. What he'd needed was a family and a woman's faith, and she'd been free with both. Through all their struggling times, she bore his children and raised them proper—all but Josie were growed now and off on their own—and even when he'd finally worked his way up to something like prosperity, and all of a sudden got the notion to give up everything for the wilds of Colorado, she hung with him. If Nathan Meeker got a dream in his head, Arvilla Delight made it her dream as well. She sat there twixt Noah and me nigh unto an hour, speaking in that soft flat voice of hers of the man she'd wed, the words filled with caring for him, and something akin to reverence.

Now this here agency was but one more dream of his—a chance to work his way out of debt, but also a way to do good by the poor Indians. "Nathan will surely take you around to see his handiwork," she said to me. "It's been hard, this year and a half we've been here. Nobody knows how hard. But my, no one thought he could do half of what he's done."

The building we were in was the agency boardinghouse, where the workers took their meals and lodging. Arvilla told me we'd be welcome to stay here for as long as it took Noah to mend and for us to get done whatever business we had to do. The tariff was four dollars a week for each of us, meals included.

Just how long we'd have to wait on old Noah wasn't clear. At this juncture I was hoping he'd survive. As for cutting Pa's trail, I wasn't much sure about that, either. But after Josie and her ma cleared out of the room, in came Bill Nunan, and first thing he says is that he's been talking with Meeker and asking about Wolf Miller.

I said, "What did you find out?"

"What I found out is that the Dutchman's out hunting antelope back there towards North Park—about where the three of us just come from."

"No."

"Yessir, scout. And he ain't due back for a week, maybe longer. So either we can sit here and whittle on sticks or we can turn right around and head back there, like I wanted to in the first place."

Well, from that little speech I got a measure of Bill's concern for Noah. But the main thing was for me to think it through in a straight line. What I come up with was this.

"Bill, we're gonna whittle on sticks." I hung fire a spell and watched his face get red. "We got Noah hurtin' and we got no clues to where Pa might be. A week from now Noah's gonna be a sight better and Wolf Miller will be on hand to straighten all this out. I don't see no choice but to set right here."

"We could go," Bill said. "We could leave Noah with this Josie girl. She can handle this business better than we can."

I said, "He ain't your kin."

"What if the Dutchman don't know where your pa's at?"

I said, "We'll deal with it."

"You ain't the one sitting out there by your claim, waitin' on us."

"Don't seem like you are either. It's my kin, Bill."

"Listen, boy, you ain't bein' sensible. We're gonna lose everything whilst you sit here."

"Bill," I said, and I held out my hand for to shake his, "you seem right concerned over my father. I appreciate it."

"Dammit, Tory!" he shouted. "I saved your tail more than once."

"You sayin' I owe you something, Bill?"

I reckon it was out in the open now so he just owned up to it. "You might say that."

"What is it I owe you, Bill?" I reached around into my war bag and fetched forth that wad of bills I had. I pulled off the hundred dollars I'd earned on the Great Western Trail, and tossed the rest onto the floor.

"That there's five hundred dollars," I said. " 'Bout what you'd make in five cattle drives. So why don't you just take it and we'll call us even."

Bill looked down at the roll of bills and I thought I saw him wrasslin' with a decision.

"Go ahead," I said. "It's money I made when you cheated at cards."

Those were shootable words in any man's company— words I might not have said if Bill had been wearing his gun. I'd pressed him just about as hard as I ought to. It was up to him to call me on it or to back down. But he just went loosey of a sudden and said, "You and I ain't had much rest lately. What you said just now—I'm gonna chalk it up to lack of sleep." He grinned again, real level. "Else I might like to kill you."

I was about ready to let him try. I'd won this one, though, so I just let him walk out of there to go lick his wounds.

Sooner or later we'd tangle—leastways that was the way I saw it. I laid my head back down, and the next thing I know it's the following morning.

There was big commotion going on downstairs—plenty of grumbling voices and a lot of banging on the floor like you might hear if folks were kicking their shoes off. I didn't even pause to pull on my boots, but rushed downstairs in my socks—and when I'm halfway down the stairs there's a whole pile of shoes laying right there in the hallway.

And Godamighty but the place is full of Indians, all of them standing around making hostile noises, not a one of 'em wearing shoes or mocassins or any other sort of footgear. In the middle of all of this there's Nathan Meeker—tallest man in the room, straight as a ramrod in a starched shirt and collar—and he's taking the worst of it from this big old Indian who might not be as tall as him but is about three times bigger around. This Ute is bruiting up to him bigger than life, decked out in a gaudy pink and black Mexican shirt and a big black felt hat with a feather in the band.

"Wear shoes three days," he says. "Wear no more."

Meeker holds up his palm and he says, "Now, Colorow. Shoes make good sense. You can't do farm work without good sturdy shoes, and I sent all the way to St. Louis for these."

From what I can tell, they've been around on this twice or three times previous. Colorow's losing patience. He picks up one of the shoes and waves it in Meeker's face. "Hurt toes," he shouts. "Make feet smell like shit."

This fetches forth a lot of like-minded murmuring from Colorow's friends. Looking down on this from where I stand, I'm thinking to myself it's a rowdy bunch of Indians we got here. I'm taking it all in, but there's no telling if things are dangerous or not.

Meeker waits for the commotion to settle down and he says, "My friend, I understand your reluctance to abandon your traditions. But if you and your brothers are going to pursue white men's occupations, you're going to have to accept white men's customs. White men wear shoes."

Colorow just kind of grunts and shifts his gaze around, and it settles on me.

He says, "Him white man. Him no wear shoes."

There was no explaining. Meeker just looked over my way like I was one more problem he didn't need.

Colorow, though, by this point he's plumb tickled with himself, translating all this into Ute for the others. This is what passes for Indian hilarity. Colorow looks at Meeker one last time and points in my direction. He says, "You give him shoes. Him *real* white man."

More translating, more backslapping on the Indian side, and the whole outfit shuffles out of there.

Now that they were gone, it was real quiet. I said, "Mr. Meeker, I just got out of bed."

"That's all right, son. Come on down here."

We shook hands and got the introductions aside, and I helped him pick up all the shoes and carry them into his office. He said, "Can you imagine preferring a pair of moccasins to some good sturdy work shoes? I'll never understand these people."

"Well, I reckon they've got their ways," I said.

"That's the problem in a nutshell, lad. They've got their ways. I'm finding that talking sense to them gets you only so far." For a moment he stopped sorting through the shoes and looked me in the eye. "I've made progress here, but it would be a trial for any man."

"Your wife has told me something of it."

"Oh, she has? Well, bless her. I'll have to take you around

the place after you've had your breakfast. How is that companion of yours?"

By the sound of it, you'd have thought Meeker hadn't been there in the kitchen and hadn't come down with a case of the faints. "He's doing better," I said. "Miss Josie and Mrs. Meeker have been tending to him."

"Well, while he mends we'll see if you can be helpful around here. Need work?"

This was one of the only times in my life I didn't, considering the money I had stashed in my war bag. But it would help pass the time, so I said yes.

"Good," he says. "There's plenty to do." By now he was stacking all the shoes over to one side of his desk. "And speaking of that, I've got correspondence to attend to that will not wait. I hope you'll excuse me."

I reckoned he was dismissing me, so I obliged and headed upstairs. Back in the room I found Josie setting by Noah's bedside with a bowl of broth.

"Best thing for him," she said. "I think he'll be all right."

My uncle laid there about half awake and half not. He looked pretty rung out. Before long he fell asleep again.

Josie looked awful pretty. It was the kind of pretty you might have to be nineteen to understand—pretty in the way that makes a feller feel kind of mournful inside. I knew I was up against it. When she stood up she about come up to my shirt pocket. She might have been my age, surely no more'n that. She pulled her hair back in a bun, like all women did, but it caught the light like amber. She had fine features and small bones. Not at all someone I'd imagine all bloodied up and sweaty, wielding a saw on a man's arm. Yet she'd done it.

"I owe you a lot, Miss Josie."

She was pouring water over by the washbasin. "I'm a nurse."

"I reckon it's like anything, ma'am. There's all kinds of nurses."

Turned out as she spoke that she had other jobs as well. She was in the government's pay as the agency schoolteacher. And she ran this boardinghouse on her pa's behalf. It was her way of pitching in to help pay off his debts.

So we had something in common, Josie Meeker and me. Each of us had a pa in need of us—only Josie was doing her share and as yet I hadn't made a dent. I told her what it was that brung me and Noah here, and about Bill Nunan tagging along. I even showed her Pa's letter.

"So you fear that he may be in danger?"

"I'm hopin' otherwise," I said. "But I expect it was Utes that burned Tourmaline and run us out of the hills thereabouts. Could be Pa's rubbed up against 'em by now."

She said, "Don't you fear for him, Mr. Bowhunter. At least, don't fear over the Utes. They're a gentle people. There's not a Ute who would raise a weapon against whites—unless he was attacked by them first."

I laughed a bit. "That Colorow and the rest didn't look too gentle to me, ma'am. Fact, it looked for a spell like your pa was out there on the high wire. They could've hurt him."

Josie's face turned sorrowful. "There are different ways to hurt people," she said. "Colorow and the others hurt my father every day, and they've never laid a hand on him."

I was about to inquire as to what she meant, for the way Josie said it told me there was considerable more going on at the White River Agency than a dispute over mocassins and work shoes. But I only got two or three words put together when in through the open door walks this Indian. Easy as you please, no knock on the doorframe, just in walks this Indian like he owns the place.

He's got this solemn way about him. He says to Josie, "I am told of your courage."

Josie lit up. She said, "Mr. Bowhunter, this gentleman is Nicaagat, a chief among the White River Utes. Nicaagat, I'd like you to meet Mr. Tory Bowhunter."

This here was one mighty impressive Ute. Dressed in

buckskins like a scout, the usual earrings and necklace and oily black braids, but large handsome features, with high cheekbones and a jaw that looked carven out of rock. His skin was the color of a new copper kettle. His eyes were deep-set, wary. He wore two knives in his belt.

He said, "You fancy shot, huh?"

"How's that?"

"You shoot straight with bow and arrow?"

I said, " 'Fraid I don't know the pointy end from the feathers. It's just a name, Bowhunter is."

He let out a small grunt and turned away. Of a sudden, I felt small and stupid. Amongst Indians a man is his name. And here I was, telling him my name meant nothing—even to me.

Nicaagat asked Josie how Noah'd hurt his arm—like Josie had been with him instead of me. Josie said it was Comanches that done it. Nicaagat turned my way again.

"No Comanches in Kansas. Cheyenne maybe," he said.

"You run into many Cheyenne?"

He said they'd used to, in the days when he and other Ute braves would cross the Front Range to hunt the buffalo. The Utes had had many a tussle with the Cheyenne over who'd hunt what.

"Well," I said, casual-like, "there ain't much cause remainin' for that. The buffaloes are gone."

Until that moment Nicaagat's face had been about as blank as an egg. It was the mask most every Indian wears before the white man, hiding their thoughts. But when I mentioned buffaloes, Nicaagat looked at me and his face filled with hate. His eyes burned.

The first thought that sprung into my head was that I was unarmed.

CHAPTER 8

"HERE," Josie said. "Let me see your hands."

Me and the Indian were locked up in a staring contest. But when Josie spoke, his fire kind of glimmered. She took aholt of his hands. They were pretty well tore up.

She said to me, "Nicaagat had an accident while handling a bale of barbed wire."

"You fix hands up good," Nicaagat said. "Better than squaw."

She looked up at him, then down at his hands again. She held them, touching the palms with her fingertips, studying his dried-up cuts. I hoped it was only that she was a nurse made her act so tender. Deep down I feared different.

I was working up a fire in the belly for this Ute. He acted superior. It would have rubbed me wrong enough was he a white man. But he had him a way with Josie, which made it plenty worse. And there was something even tougher to take. It was that I knew, in some ways at least, that he really was superior. Some men just carry weight, no matter what color.

They spoke about this and that, Josie and him, till I got the feeling there weren't much I could add to the proceedings, unless I wanted to poke my nose in and maybe stir up a fight. I was amind to, but I knew that wouldn't buy me much, other than to make me look like a jealous fool. Which, of course, I was. But I had just enough sense to know it and get out of there.

Which ain't to say I wasn't gonna feel low and mean over it. Plenty low, and plenty mean.

I wasn't sure just what I'd walked into here at White River. Two days before I'd had me one set of problems, and now I was working on new ones. I pondered that walking down the stairs. I would've set on the front porch to mope properly but it was coated with Utes. They looked at me cross-eyed. I looked back. There was a whole lot more Indians around this place than there were white people. But at least this bunch didn't make my hair stand on end like Nicaagat.

I walked around, looked in on Temper at the stable, and then the dinner bell clanged.

The hands who worked the place for Nathan Meeker were all boys from Greeley. Meeker'd brung most of their folks west when he founded that town. There were eight altogether. Shadrach Price was the oldest and the only one that was married. Him and the rest were all around the table, and so was his wife Flora Ellen. She had two little ones and they added to the commotion. Bill Nunan was also on hand. By the sound of his halloo, you'd of thought we were still partners.

Bill had spent the morning planting fence posts and stringing bobwire. He said, "Rough stuff to deal with."

"Worse'n that," Shad said, and one or two others said, "Amen."

"I'd have guessed that was the Indians' to do," I said. "They're the ones that'll gain by it."

Shad said, "Gain by what?"

"Why, the bobwire, the canal, all that. It's their farm you're working on."

"It's Meeker's farm." The one who spoke was Arthur Thompson. He was a stringy sort. He wore spectacles and his hair stuck up like porcupine quills. "The Utes will eat what he grows on it, but it's us'll do the work. Been that way since we got here."

"Art's a veteran," Shad said. "Been here the whole eighteen months."

"The only one who has," Thompson said. "You all are just pups."

That struck him funny and he laughed. Turns out he was right, after a fashion. There wasn't a man at the table as old as me, save Bill, and most of them hadn't been on hand more than two or three months. I asked what happened to the ones what come before.

Thompson said, "Most got scared and left."

"Hell," Frank Dresser said. "These bucks'll make noise but they won't hurt ya." He was the youngest of them and the gamest. "Let 'em ride their horses and they're happy."

"Then I reckon," I said, "they ain't happy about that wire you're stringing."

"Probably ain't," Thompson said.

I said, "What about this feller Nicaagat?"

"You mean Jack?" Thompson said. "He was reared with white folks, you know. His name was Jack Norton till he come back here."

Shad said, "You still might want to call him Nicaagat."

"Well, what about him?" I said. "What about Jack?"

Shad said, "You tell 'em."

Thompson leaned across the table. "The other day? When the freighters come in? The old man's watching 'em unload the wagon and Jack comes walkin' by with some of his friends. All of a sudden-like the old man doesn't want nothing unloaded, like he's hiding something. So of course Jack walks over and pulls off the tarpaulin and sees these bales of bobwire. Enough bobwire to fence in most of Powell Park."

"Well, you should of seen it," Dresser said. "Weren't but a couple of us seen it. You seen it, Shad?"

"Sure did," Shadrach said.

"Seen what?" I said.

"Jack," Thompson said, raising both his hands, "Jack picked up a bale of wire in his bare hands, lifted the thing over his head and heaved it at the old man."

"Did he hit him?"

"A sixty-pound bale of wire? Hard enough to lift it, let alone aim it at no one." He grinned kinda sly. "Come right close, though."

Bill said, "What happened then?"

"He just stalked off," Frank said. "The Indian, that is. The old man held his ground. Just set his jaw like that." He did a fair imitation.

I said, "Does Josie know about this?"

Thompson said, "My guess is she don't."

Then someone behind me said, "I'd rather she didn't."

I reckon in the general clamor of things no one had noticed him come in, and no one knew how long he'd been there.

Thompson wasn't smiling anymore. He said, "Hello, Mr. Meeker."

The old man waved it all off. "We won't fret the ladies with this sort of thing," he said. "One day our Indian brothers will see the light and help us to help them. That is a certainty."

One of the Greeley boys said, "Sure they will, sir." But things were kind of quiet in there.

Old Meeker was jolly now. "It's you I've come for, young Bowhunter." He laid a hand on my shoulder. "I promised you a tour of our little utopia. Now come along."

When we got out into the daylight, I told him to hang fire a minute while I run upstairs. I slunk into the room real quiet so's not to wake Noah. I got down on all fours and reached under my bed for my war bag, and from out of it I drew my gunbelt and a box of cartridges. I set down on the edge of the bed and shook some out and filled my Colt. I spun the cylinder and clicked it shut.

"Is it that Indian?" Uncle Noah's eyes were on me. From that I gathered that he must have been more awake that morning than Josie or me had thought.

I said, "Just playing it safe, Uncle." I felt him watching me while I tightened the belt and strapped the holster down. I didn't look up, but I said, "I'm glad you're alive, Noah."

It needn't have been said. Like as not it embarrassed him. But by God too much goes unspoken with them you love. I learned that early.

I got up to go. He said, "Tread easy, son. She likes him."

So he'd heard plenty. Maybe he'd even heard something after I'd left Josie and that Indian together, and he knew more about things between them than I did. I thought of Josie with her yellow hair. It ain't so, I thought. Can't be.

Nathan Meeker clucked to the team and we headed out past the livery stable and the warehouse. "Josie tells me you're a friend of Wood Gettys," he said. "You should have told me."

"Yessir. I met him playing poker on the way to Denver."

"That so? The last time I played poker with Wood Gettys was thirty years ago. Did you win?"

"Yessir, I come out ahead."

"You don't say?" He laughed. "Wood must have liked you."

"Guess I just got lucky."

"Lad, when you play poker with Wood Gettys, luck is irrelevant."

I grinned at him. "He said to pass along his regards to you and the missus."

"Yes, Arvilla always did have a soft spot for the scoundrel." His voice had that way about it, like he was thinking of things long previous to this. "The truth is, we were both promising young men, Wood and I. Both of us a bit full of ourselves. But I took the path of principle, and I'm afraid brother Gettys strayed onto the path of commerce. Rich men end up dabbling in politics, which they use as a means of getting richer."

"Is that how it is with Wood?" I said.

"Well, I've read that our friend is chairman of 'The Governor's Citizens' Committee on the Resolution of the Ute Indian Problem.' I'll venture that didn't hurt his chances of getting the freight contract."

The world continued to amaze me.

Then Meeker said, "It's not that I judge him. I just suppose I hoped more might come of him."

Well, thinking back to the stories Gettys had told me that night on the Kansas-Pacific, plenty had come of him. He'd seen most of the country—helped open up a fair share of it himself—and he'd faced dangers, courted beautiful women, and made fortunes on both oceans. If it took a bit of straying onto the path of commerce to get wealthy and ride in palace cars, I was prepared to do my share if it come to that.

Meeker drove the buckboard through the agency streets and pointed out each building and what it was made for. They weren't fancy things—just simple wooden buildings with everyday uses—but he'd designed each one of them himself, and parceled out the land for them, and run the construction work and accounted for every nail. The whole agency was made up of maybe a dozen buildings—sheds and milkhouse included—but it was made in the image of Nathan C. Meeker.

That's what he wanted for his Utes, too—to make them over in his image. He laid it out for me, how he knew the old ways were doomed by the great tide of the white man, and how these Utes could be saved from the fate of the other Indians—but only if they'd change. The White River Utes would take on white men's ways, or they'd get took off their homeland and put in pens like their cousins. Meeker was one white man who would admit that treaties really meant nothing when white men offered them to red men. He told me there was no fighting that, but if you were a smart Indian, you could work it so that when the wave finally come breakin' over you, you didn't get washed clean away.

We crossed one of the irrigation ditches at Arvilla Bridge. Past that it was a good mile to the lodges of Chief Douglas and his followers. In the fields around us, there must have been five hundred ponies.

"There's half my problem," Meeker said. "The Utes care more for these blasted horses than they do for anything else."

"They're good-looking horses," I said. I liked the sight of them, so many spread out over bottomland—the river winding along through the willows on the south side, the Danforth Hills all blue-grey with sage to the west and north, and great blown masses of clouds overhead. We were downwind from the Ute village. You could smell the wood smoke, and if you cocked an ear you heard the shouts of children.

"The horse was placed on this earth as a tool for man's use," the old man said. "These Indians treat it as an object of worship." A hard edge come into his voice, like it was the ponies' fault. "You cannot convince them otherwise. All you can do is act with firmness and in their best interests. Turn them in some other direction."

"What do you mean, sir?"

"Modern pursuits," he said. "Agricultural science. Orchards to raise peaches and apples. Wool growing and cattle breeding. Chicken farming. Forestry. The hills upriver are covered with pine to make lumber. And mining—there's coal in these hills. Gold perhaps. Silver. If industry took root here, lad, the road from Rawlins would be graded, perhaps tracks would be laid. And when white settlers finally arrived in numbers, the Utes would be in a position to prosper from it." He shook his head. "Instead, it's horses. Always these horses."

I begun to gather that Meeker had been through this a time or two previous. He told me that the first Ute agency had been built ten miles downriver, and that when he'd got the job of Indian agent some eighteen months before, the first thing he did was move the whole shootin' match to this location. His reason was that here was the place the Utes grazed their herds. He hoped to cut down on the number of horses by cutting down the amount of land they could graze on.

"Did they go for that?"

"I cannot say they cared much for it, lad—but Indians don't always know what's best for them. If they did, when we white men first encountered them, we would not have found them running about all but naked, painting themselves to look like birds and wolves. It has been my intention to guide them out of savagery. Many have tried to thwart me—not least of them that fellow Nicaagat. But I will prevail. That is a certainty."

I couldn't much fault him for good intentions. He had more sympathy for these Indians than any white man I'd listened to—and it was a sight better in my book to hear this stuff of his than all that other business about the Utes having to go. Still and all, I couldn't help but get a queasy feeling about the old man's state of mind. You could hear it in his voice—like he'd taken the Utes for his children. He thought they ought to love him for it, and treat him like a wise old father—and they didn't. What come through was the bitterness of a man whose love wasn't returned.

It was just about then we caught sight of some of the Greeley boys running hard over the field. It was Dresser and Thompson and two of the others. Meeker drew the reins and we watched them run toward us, Dresser pressing his floppy felt hat down with his hand.

Meeker called out to ask of them what the trouble might be.

"It's the fence posts, sir," Thompson said. He was breathing hard, his Adam's apple bobbing like a cork. "They're down."

"What's that you say?"

"Somebody pulled 'em up. If they couldn't pull one up, they just clipped the wire off."

Meeker got to his feet beside me, hoping to see better, but there weren't much to see for all the ponies in the way.

He said, "Every one of them?"

"Nearly all, sir," Dresser said. "Sixty are down, the rest unstrung."

"This happened while you were at dinner?"

Dresser nodded. "We got back out there just now and saw what they done. They was quick about it."

Meeker set his jaw and gazed out toward the lodges. He set back down and said, "You boys are going back out there to reset those posts."

All of them looked from one to the other and I don't reckon they were too eager to go.

"I'll see Douglas about this," Meeker said. "We'll talk. None of you are in the least jeopardy." He smiled. "Now off you go, lads."

The wondrous thing is that they went. I watched them plod back through the field. It said plenty about their faith in the old man. Me, I might have thought two or three times before heading out there without a weapon.

He said to me, "I'm afraid I won't have time to drive you back to the compound."

I thought, Hell, I wouldn't miss this, and asked if I could tag along. We drove northward around the herd so as not to raise a stir. Meeker talked as we went, but it was a strange sort of muttering talk, like I was listening in on his thoughts. He said he couldn't understand it, never been worse baffled. They'd disagreed before, him and Douglas. They'd bargained and parlayed and negotiated every which way since the day Meeker'd got there. But the old chief had never been rancorous. He might have begged off on doing what he didn't want to see done, but he had never just come out and destroyed property. No, this is different. A change now, the stakes changing. *What about my family? Violence cannot be allowed to take root in this valley. I will not have it. I shall warn Douglas against this sort of thing. Douglas will heed my warning.*

And before I knew it, we were looking Douglas right in the eye.

He was all chief, hair almost white but the body still deep-chested and hard, and set into that bronze hawk's face a pair of bright hazel eyes, almost gold. Round like cat's eyes, but sharper, watchful. There was a white man somewhere in the family tree—probably some trapper who'd took himself a squaw one or two generations back.

He'd come out of his tepee with a handful of followers—one of them the same big hombre Colorow that led the fuss over the shoes. There wasn't nothing funny about Colorow now. He'd changed his duds—no more Mexican shirt—and all that painted skin and porcupine-quill jewelry gave the impression this was a serious Indian. I caught his glance one time, and I knew right then it was him and his cronies that tore up the fence posts.

Meeker got down from the buckboard and him and Douglas traded greetings. I stayed up top so's to see better. We were well nigh surrounded by Utes—elders and young braves bunched around, naked young'uns wrassling one another and chasing through the dust. Right by us a few squaws were stretching hides. They looked us up and down real slow, but their hands kept working.

I cast about for Jack but he wasn't to be seen. I should have known it, for they'd told me at dinner that him and Douglas had little truck with each other. Jack thought it was time a younger man took over. He had his own band upriver a few miles—maybe three dozen tepees by the mouth of Coal Creek Canyon. It was poorer pasture thereabouts, but Jack—him and the young studs that run with him—could flex their muscles without the headman eyeing 'em all the time.

Douglas looked Meeker level in the eye, and he had dignity to match the old agent and wit besides. Douglas had himself something else, too. He had his own land beneath his feet. It was something you just read in him. He knew this soil was his. He believed it as simple and as sure as he believed in his own life.

Him and Meeker got through discussing the weather—appeared the dry spell might never end, appeared that fall might be late—and then Meeker got round to the point.

"I'm having some trouble with my fence posts, Douglas. Seems they won't stay in the ground."

Things grew so quiet I could hear a meadowlark down by the river.

"Perhaps the wind blows them down."

"Then the wind also cuts fence wire."

Douglas said something in Ute to Colorow, and Colorow turned to one of the braves behind him, motioned over yonder with his arm and give him some sort of order.

The chief spoke to Meeker again. Kind of casual-like, he said, "This wire you string. What is the purpose of this wire?"

"Now, Douglas," Meeker said. "I've told you all about it before. Our cattle and sheep need grass to themselves. We cannot set aside the best pasture in this valley for ponies—not if you and I are to establish a well-balanced farming community, run on modern agricultural principles, for the benefit of all your tribe."

Nice speech, I thought. But Douglas said, "My braves say you wish to harm my horses."

The old man shook his head. "The cows and sheep we've brought into Powell Park will feed you and your families, and the beef and the wool you sell in Rawlins will help bring prosperity to this valley." He kind of rotated as he talked—preaching, I guess you'd say. He had his palms outstretched and he smiled. "No longer will you need to leave this reservation and roam the valleys of the Bear and the Little Snake and up into North Park for game. This patch of earth will be your home. All you require you will raise yourselves, right here. And there will be less need for ponies."

The way the congregation just kinda stood there, I got the feeling none of 'em savvied a word that Meeker said. Just then the brave that Colorow had spoke to led a horse out from between the tepees.

This one was a beauty, a big-barreled stallion. Chestnut he was, a full hand to the better of most Indian ponies I'd run across. But he was hurt. He was cut up through the loins something frightful—so bad he couldn't hardly lead, so bad it turned my stomach to see. The blood had run down between his legs and the dust had stuck to it, and there was plenty more cuts and torn flesh along inside his hind legs where he'd fought to get free.

Barbed wire will do that.

I looked at Meeker and I saw him turn color, the way he'd done when he'd first seen Noah's arm. I reckon blood didn't set well with Nathan Meeker—just plain took the starch out of him. All the pretty words, the clever words like he was prone to deal in—they didn't count for much in the sight of blood.

Douglas's eyes took in the sight of that horse. He touched it on the neck and withers. I could see the rage flicker across his face, but he kept a tight rein. It took a lot of strength for a man to hold himself in like this Douglas did.

He turned back from his horse and straightened his whole frame and looked at Meeker. "My friend, you will string no more wire in this valley."

That about said it. Meeker stood there swaying, like a man who'd been struck a blow. He stammered out something about how unfortunate it was that Douglas's horse got cut up, and how even the best intentions sometimes lead to accidents and suchlike, but even as he spoke he was backing toward me and the buckboard, and when we'd dusted out of there it come to me that Meeker wasn't the one that had gave out a warning today. Douglas was.

CHAPTER 9

TIME was, three or four years previous, I might've gone either way, good or bad. I'd run off from that school Pa'd sent me to in New Orleans. It wasn't that I didn't learn nothing. It's just that I was used to the range. So like I say I run off from that school and got a job on a fishing boat outside of Delacroix. I was fifteen or so and in with bad company.

One night I got cut up in a fight. This warehouseman told me my nose looked Mexican and he didn't like Mexicans. He tried to remove it with a large knife. He failed in that, but before I knocked him out he managed to open up my face a few times. I drug myself back to the docks, but I'd bled so much I couldn't make it to the boat. I wakened at daybreak with my head throbbing fierce and two of my ribs busted, and when I lifted my head it was from a pool of old fish heads and scullery water out back of a bar. It was just Tory Bowhunter and a bunch of cats in that alley. I knew right then it was time to get back to Texas.

I told Josie all about that, as she'd asked me about the scars on my face. I told her how I'd managed to get back to Corpus Christi, and how Noah turned out to be working a ranch twenty miles in from there, and how he grabbed me up like some wayward cub and said I was going to straighten out or he'd kill me himself.

He worked my tail off, and when I wasn't working cows in the warm weather he had me bust horses. One of them he chose himself. It would be mine, but I'd gentle-break it he said, the way the Indians do. It takes longer and it'll sap a man's patience something grievous, but you'll get a good horse. He'd chose me the toughest young mustang colt I'd ever saw, with bite marks on his neck from fighting out on the range, one that other bronc fighters had come close to ruining with the quirt for having too much piss and vinegar in his veins. I recall them hours in the corral, that beast fighting me every inch of the way, like he'd rather die than trust a man, and me coming well-nigh close to hating him, and Noah leaning over the plank fence half laughing and telling me not to cuss so much and saying, "Temper, temper."

I told Josie plenty things about my life—stuff I hadn't much pondered before, let alone spoke to no one. She told me about herself, too, her growing up among all them free-thinking folks in Ohio and New York and Greeley, with all their crazy ideas about utopias and eating only vegetables and having free love. That free love part I found a specially good subject for thought.

I come to think Josie Meeker might be smarter than me. I wouldn't have told no other man. Yet I kind of fancied the notion. It made me think of her different-like, and it made me want to know her more. I'd spent my time with men—cowhands and buffalo men and fishermen and whatnot—and I'd picked up a lot of hearsay. For all I savvied of 'em, most womenfolk might have dropped down from the moon.

I showed Josie the buffalo tail I always carried in my war bag. She wanted to know everything about my buffalo days.

"Wasn't it horrible to you," she said, "slaughtering thousands of innocent creatures?"

I told her it was what me and Pa done for a living. "Anyhow," I said, "there was so many of 'em out on the prairie, you never thought the Lord would miss a few here and there."

Well, that sounded pretty lame. I knew it just as soon as I said it. Josie's eyes didn't waver none off of mine, nor did she say nothing, but it was like she spoke to me. I'd never faced up to it before, the weight of all that killing. Maybe Pa did sicken of it like Sarie Clement said. I could savvy that.

Them hours Josie and me spent together, I got to thinking much more on things than many a cowhand is prone to. In the morning I'd help dig Meeker's new canal—it was the job least likely to get me shot by some Ute, so I liked it. I'd work that shovel and I'd think of her. Then late in the day, when Josie'd finished up school teaching and tending to business at the boardinghouse, she'd come upstairs to look in on Noah. Sometimes we'd sit with him. But other times we'd tell him how much he needed his rest, and me and Josie would go out on the porch and set. I got to craving those times— 'specially during the night when I was alone by the window. I'd see the stars glistening out yonder in the darkness, far distant from this little agency and the big looming hills and the whole Godamighty complicated world, and I'd crave her company.

Not that it was always pleasurous. We disagreed on a thing or two—mainly Jack.

"You might at least refer to him by his name," she said.

"I do. Jack."

"His name is Nicaagat."

"I kind of fancy Jack. Jack Norton. Got a nice sound to it."

She said, "Do you know what he calls you? 'Nameless One.' He says it's hard to call you Bowhunter if you're not sure it applies."

I said, "Why do you listen to that Indian?"

"That Indian is a chief," she said. "He spent most of his life in the white man's world and chose to return and lead his own people. There is great courage and dignity in him. And besides, I find him rather gallant."

I hoped that was all she found him.

Noah's fever departed in a few days. He was weak as a babe but on the mend. A week passed and he could still scarcely lift what was left of his arm, but his eyes were growing bright and he ate like the chuck was free.

One time he was scarfing down supper and I said to Josie, "I'm still stuck with this old bear, thanks to you."

She said, "Tory Bowhunter, you love this old bear. I'm growing fond of him myself."

Noah just looked sour-like at both of us and kept on eating.

Next day was Sunday and in the afternoon me and Josie went down by White River. I wore my long-roweled Mexican silver spurs and my best and fanciest embroidered cowboy shirt that cost me nigh unto ten dollars once in San Antonio. It had little red diamondy things on the shoulders and they went with my bandanna. I wore my hat kind of slaunchwise and I thought I looked pretty slick.

I didn't wear my six-gun for Josie asked me not to. I wasn't eager to venture forth unarmed among the Indians, but I was eager to please Josie if she wanted it that way. She said no Ute would harm her or any friend of hers.

There was a huge old willow a little distance up from the river that had got struck by lightning. The big wide limbs were long since dead and blanched white but it stood there like a rock. Josie explained as how Douglas considered it big medicine and had Ahutupuwit lay out his racing strip so's the old tree was the finish point. The strip itself was a plain dirt straightaway running about a half-mile along the riverside. You could tell that the Utes took care to tend it well.

I tied the horses to the willow and Josie and me walked over by the water. The box elders grew thick on the bank, tangled in with chokecherries and one or two red willows. In the shade alongside them, Josie spread a cloth and fetched out biscuits and cherry jam. It was cool and beautiful thereabouts. The sky was bluer than turquoise, and the clouds looked like they'd been painted in for show. Across the river to the southward, Roan Plateau lay huge and quiet, like something alive but sleeping, and the shadows of clouds moved over its flanks as lazy as a yawn.

All that come into my head to say was that the jam was tart.

"Well," she said, "I'm very sorry."

So she'd made the damn jam. I said, "Tart jam's fine. I favor tart jam."

That was my stab at conversation and considering my lack of success with it I reckoned to retreat for a spell. We just laid there and listened to the river murmuring past. Just to lay about with Josie was not a bad way to beguile the time.

Then she said, "Do you know much about hummingbirds, Tory?"

I'd never seen a hummingbird and wouldn't have known one if it was served on a plate. I told her so and she got to her feet. Damn if she didn't point out a hundred hummingbirds making commotion up there in the box elders.

I said, "Sure are itty-bitty things."

She got all dreamy and female over them. "Aren't they lovely? Like little figurines brought to life."

I didn't say much on that, except I recollect thinking it would take a handful of them to make a meal. Josie was up on her tiptoes peering round for them.

The fact is that I was considerable less interested in hummingbirds than I was in Josie Meeker. Watching the little busters go zipping through the branches was restful enough. Their wings made a pleasurous sound and they had a funny knack of looking one way and flitting the other. But Josie's sunbonnet was the color of a dove's breast, and the hair that wisped out from under there was the color of honey, and her eyes had a way of looking into yours and then away. A man is nineteen but once. At nineteen it ain't hummingbirds that stir his heart.

The wind kicked up of a sudden and begun to blow Josie's skirts. They flattened up against her legs and I quietly praised God for it. I wished I'd have known more then about women. She was surely waiting on me to kiss her. Instead I talked. "You like it much here at the agency?"

She still seemed kind of up there with the hummingbirds. "I've never been so happy in my life."

"Josie, I got to tell you that there's trouble brewin' here. There's plenty sign of it all around us."

That broke the spell sure enough. She plopped down cross-legged before me and clenched her hands in her lap. "If there's trouble coming," she said, "it's because of white men."

"The Utes may of had somethin' to do with it."

That got her back up. "Tory Bowhunter," she said, "the Utes that seem so unsympathetic to you are a brave, generous people who were here a long time before white men. A long time before the trappers and greedy prospectors who covet their land, a long time before the soldiers who crave the killing of them and their wives and babies. A long time, too, before the do-gooders who think they can make them over in their own image, like God made Adam."

"You'd think I started it."

She said, "I'm sorry. It's not you."

Then it come to me who she thought it was. "It's your father."

"No."

But I knew different. I said, "I won't let on."

Our eyes met. She was deciding whether to share her secret with me. "He means well," she said. "He really does. He knows what happens to Indians. When the white man comes, the Indians end up dead or in exile. I know he's hoping to save them—they're 'his' Indians—by turning them into white men. He wants them to build irrigation canals. And wear boots while they dig. And live in wooden houses, and grow pretty gardens, and stay here tending cattle instead of riding out for antelope."

She raised up and walked out toward the meadow. Where she stood was the finest pasture in Powell Park. Hereabouts, in betwixt the racing strip and Douglas's village, most of the ponies belonging to the White River Utes stood cropping the grass.

She said, "Do you know what horses mean to these people?"

I shrugged. "I know Indians like horses."

She was looking out over the valley, not at me. "It's more than that, Tory. Much more—it's worship. A Ute's horse is his pride, it's what makes him manly."

She launched into a little lesson all about the history of the Utes—about how early on they'd been pushed around by the other tribes, never having a patch of land to call their own or a place to hunt without fear, and then come onto horses. Some of this I'd heard from Noah—how the Utes had growed to be the finest of all Indian horsemen, and how they'd earned the respect of the other tribes by whompin' them on horseback. If a Ute warrior had to choose between feeding his wives or his horses, he wouldn't have to think twice.

Josie said, "Horses make up his manhood. How could a brave turn his ponies into plow horses? Why would he want to?"

"Sooner or later, I reckon he'll have to."

She thought on it. Then she said, "I know."

I felt so tender toward her. I got up and put my arms around Josie Meeker and felt how small and warm she was. She lifted her face to mine and just the look of her was enough.

Her secret wasn't so terrible after all. She thought her father was wrong and the Utes were right. She knew the more the old man tried to help them in his wrongheaded way, the more they'd hate him—and still she taught school for him, and ran his boardinghouse, and nursed his workmen. Most of all she kept her doubts to herself—so that even when the time came that his pride cost him everything, he'd know he still had his Josie.

In a minute she broke away from me. I knew we were out in the open, but it was one of them moments you don't care who's watching. Douglas's village, maybe eighty tepees, was a quarter-mile up from the river bank. I looked over there.

The squaws were doing chores, mostly busy with skins—stretching them on racks or tanning them in dug-out logs. You could tell where their children were by the clouds of dust. Their sound was the far-off hollering that kids make. The men set on their haunches passing the time. By custom, Ute women did the work and Ute men enjoyed the sunshine. I could see some virtue in that.

Problem was there were too many men there. I recognized Sowerwick, Jack's henchman. I walked several paces off to one side to get a better view around the horses. Yep, it was Sowerwick—taller than most Indians and uglier, with a head like a turkey buzzard. If Sowerwick was there, Jack was there. And if Jack was there, he was there to powwow with Douglas.

It was just an uneasy feeling I had in my mind, and I felt it might be better to get Josie back toward the agency compound. But then Sowerwick sighted us. There was some pointing and palavering over yonder, and one of Sowerwick's cronies slunk into the nearest tepee and come back out with Jack.

Whatever quality it is that lets one wolf lead the pack, Jack had it. Just the way he walked told you he was the strongest, the man others follow. There were taller braves, but Jack was broadest through the chest. Even at a quarter-mile you could read the power in him. I could see how the others all turned their heads toward him, how they cleared a path for him as he moved toward his horse. It was more than muscle, even more than rank. He was just the best amongst them.

He begun to ride toward us. Sowerwick and three others fell in behind him in a V. They commenced a slow trot, wending their way through the scattering of horses. Jack wore his buckskin jumper and the fringes fluttered as he rode.

I turned toward Josie and saw her face. She was watching Jack, and she was lit up, eyes wide. A man might offer to commit murder to have a woman look at him like that. She was looking at that Ute like that—and I didn't like it much.

I wanted us out of there. Two of Jack's riders had Winchesters in hand and I was sure the others were armed. My guns were under my bed back at the boardinghouse. Even if I'd had them with me, I weren't sure that five-to-one was my best odds.

I pried Josie's attention away from that Indian and got her to help gather up the cloth and the food. By the time we were back under the dead willow where Temper and Josie's horse were hitched, our company had arrived.

Jack set bareback on his mount, like him and the pony were one animal. The horse was a pretty buckskin colt, sturdy and a trifle stubby-legged, with a good sharp eye. Jack had him by the mane and the pony blew through the nostrils, full of himself. Temper got bad signals from him and grew skittish, so I took his bridle and petted him.

Jack come about as close to cracking a smile as I'd ever seen him. "Miss Josie, you are well?"

"Yes, Nicaagat. Yes, I feel wonderful. Can't you feel fall in the air?"

He made that Indian grunt that passes for yes or no, depending. "Fall come late this year," he said. "Then cold winter. Much snow." He swept his hand northward toward the Danforth Hills, the sort of gesture a man makes over land he owns. He was right—summer would tarry a while. Josie had told me the aspens would look like they'd been hung with gold coins. But not yet.

Everyone waited on Jack to speak again. I reckoned on some parcel of authentic Indian lore—something like how the Utes were so close to nature they spoke to beavers or suchlike. So he says, all weighty and serious, "Me know about weather. Read Farmer's Almanac."

I erupted—laughed till I halfway fell over. Couldn't help it. I wanted to tell Josie her pa was making real headway with these White River folks. But I dropped a lid over it when it appeared from the faces of them on the scene that I might get shot. Josie didn't look none too pleased with me, either.

Of a sudden I noticed that a crowd was gathering. From the Douglas encampment, more braves, maybe twenty in all, were commencing to drift our way across the pasture. That sobered me up pretty quick—by which time Sowerick said to me, "You have speedy horse, this one?"

The ugly one was doing the boss's talking. Meantime Jack managed to look bored as hell, glaring off at the horizon like Tory Bowhunter wasn't worth his time. I said, "Speedy as most."

"Nicaagat say your horse slow as old woman. Him show you fast horse."

Jack was amind to show me more than that, and I knew it. What he wanted was to show me who was the better man—and to do it in front of Josie. I looked up at him. He turned his face to me real slow. I saw those wolf's eyes, looking at me like I was a meal.

"What the hell," I said.

Jack spoke something to his buzzard friend in Ute. He was plumb not gonna talk to me. When he'd finished, Sowerwick pointed for me to look down the racing strip at a big boulder down there.

He said, "Race start here. Go around rock and come back."

That was just all right with me. I said to Temper, "That all right with you?"

Jack stepped his pony toward us. I could feel my whole body coil up. But he just looked down at Josie and said, "Must ask for hat." Before I knew it, he'd reached down and tugged at the ribbon under her chin. I was ready to cut out his Indian heart. But Josie stood there looking up at him—the sun aglow on her face—and I got the feeling she didn't mind at all.

He tied the bonnet to one of the wide-branching limbs of the willow, maybe eight or nine feet off the ground, and it was plain that in a few minutes one of us would get to hand it back to the lady. I climbed up in the saddle and drew alongside Jack, and Josie stepped up between us and put a hand on each of our arms. She looked from one of us to the other, and when I saw her face it was the face of a woman getting the thrill of her young life, and I knew then that Uncle Noah'd been right and that I had myself an Indian rival and a ladylove who played a dangerous game, and I was so filled with fury that when Sowerwick shouted "Go!" I clapped the spurs to my horse and whipped his flanks like I never had and never should have and we were off like we'd been blown from a cannon.

And there, ten yards ahead, was Jack, his pony so quick off the mark I forgot my rage and come near to laughing again. The dirt flew up at us and the hoots of a couple dozen Indians filled my ears. But in no time they were behind us, and what I heard now as we tore down the track was Temper's hooves pounding the dirt and his breath coming hard and fast.

We settled into it—just Jack and me ahorseback, putting distance behind us. The Ute still led us three lengths, but he wasn't stretching it out. My horse had got his stride—hind legs digging for it, forelegs straining for more ground—and I could feel the surge of Temper's body heaving under me and the heat and the smell of sweat coming off him and I knew there was something special driving him. He'd made up his mind to run at this Indian. I just bent low on his neck and pumped him into each stride and shouted, and we commenced to close the gap.

Jack was first to reach the boulder and took the turn wide in a shower of dust, but I had a cow pony under me and we skidded round that big rock as tight as a noose and come out just a length behind. I shouted again "Hyah! Hyah!" as we straightened out and Temper got his action back, and in front of us Jack was screeching and the sound of our ponies' hoofbeats was something you felt in your ears like the pounding of your blood.

The harder Temper come at Jack, the harder his buckskin kept diggin'. We strained for an inch on him, and another inch, but like floodtide the ground rolled away from under us. And the willow tree, white as bone with the sun on it, that dove-gray bonnet dangling from it by a ribbon, got closer quick—two strides nearer to Jack's grasp than mine.

I hollered for Temper to give it more run, but that's something you got to tell your horse with your hands and your body, so I pressed into him and rolled with his stride and we come bustin' up alongside Jack's pony with two hundred yards to go. We were on his off side now and he come over on us and our flanks banged together. I decided right there to carry wide of him. If I fought him ahorseback I'd lose, and I wasn't going to lose.

We were stride for stride now—the dust flying no more in Temper's face or mine—but me and my horse were far off line. The Ute didn't come over on us again, for he saw what I saw. If both of us kept to the straight and narrow, Jack's course would take him right to the bonnet, while I'd be off by the riverbank where the hummingbirds lived. But I kept Temper wide so long even Jack must have thought we were through, and ten yards out from the finish I gave the reins a hard left-handed tug and we cut over as sharp as a crease. I put the spurs into Temper and he give me one last burst, and for an instant it appeared we might bowl the Indian over just as we got to the tree. But just as we were set to collide, I jerked Temper's head back and to the right—like I'd done a thousand times or more when we'd roped calves—and as Jack's fingers begun to close on the bonnet I reached up with my free hand and grabbed it away. The buckskin flew past and carried Jack along with it—and since Temper was planted now all I had to do to keep the bonnet was not let it go.

Jack kept going. Didn't break stride, didn't even look back. All his Ute friends let out after him, whoopin' and waving their rifles and scattering the grazing ponies before them. I set atop old Temper and watched them cut a big arc through the meadow and curl back toward Jack's lodges over by Coal

Creek Canyon. I just petted my horse's neck and watched them as they disappeared around the willows on the bend of White River, till all that remained was the far-off sound of hoofbeats.

Some time after that I learned something—that in the run of years a man will taste real victory once, maybe twice. A right, true victory comes not just when a foe is beaten, but when a foe is worth the beating. The bonnet was in my hand and I ruffled it through Temper's mane. This horse was mine and we'd taken Jack on and beat him together. In that moment I forgot Josie entirely.

Things settled down again and directly the thought of Josie come back to me. I cantered Temper round to where she stood. She was down the track a ways—staring off toward nowhere it seemed—and I confess I felt the hero. I reined up before her, slapping the bonnet on my thigh to shake off the dust, and then I bent low and held it out to her.

"You!" she said. Her cheeks were hot and red and her eyes brimmed with tears. "You shamed him!"

"Huh?"

"You shamed him. How could you?"

And with that Josie Meeker struck my leg with her little fist and stalked off toward the agency. Left me with her horse, and with our picnic basket, and with that goddamn bonnet.

Later on I come in from the stable and found Noah standing before the mirror, teaching himself how to wax his mustaches one-handed.

"You're standin' in my light," he said.

I laid down on the bed with my feet up and watched him.

"All right," he said. "How's that?" He'd managed to get one end of his mustache pointed east and the other sort of west-by-northwest.

I said, "If you was a clock you'd read about ten minutes to three."

He smiled. The first time I'd seen them gap teeth of his since he'd lost his arm. "Close enough."

He went about housekeeping at the washbasin—closing his razor, folding his towel—things a man does every day without a thought. One-handed was harder.

I said, "I raced Jack just now."

He just stared.

"Whomped him," I said.

"The hell you say."

"Don't cuss, Uncle."

He cocked his head. "You really beat him?"

"By a frog's hair, but yes."

That one big paw could still pound a nephew's back. "God dang," he said. "I'd like to of seen that." He was snorting with laughter like he'd beaten the Ute himself.

I related the whole story. He fetched forth a bottle from under the mattress and pulled the cork with his teeth.

I took a long pull and then he took one, and I took another and it went on that way for some time. He said, "That's a specially good horse you got, Tory boy."

"He is, ain't he?"

"You can handle him like nobody's business."

"That I can."

"You know what that means?" He hoisted up to his full height and said, "It means any feller that can get that range pony actin' proper, someday he'll have Josie Meeker doin' likewise."

I thought about that. I said, "Who the hell wants her actin' proper?"

He sat down. "Good point."

About then the door opened and Bill Nunan stood there.

He said, "I'm leaving."

I kind of worked him into focus. He had his Colt strapped on.

Noah said, "Well, so long."

"So long," Bill said, and out he goes.

"What was that about?" I said.

"Don't know," my uncle says. "First I heard of it."

I went to the window and saw Bill's bay hitched up to the rail out front. There was a loaded packhorse besides. I went down the stairs after him.

I caught up with him in the street, checking the cinches under the packhorse.

"What's the story here, Billy?"

He straightened up. "How's that?"

"I was wonderin' what sort of wickedness you was up to."

He looked me right in the eyeball. "And you're bent on findin' out."

I looked him right back, and I nodded slow.

"Tory boy, fact is I'm gettin' restless hereabouts waitin' on things to happen, so I reckon to do some prospecting."

I looked things over. "I don't see no pick or shovel, Bill. Not so much as a pan."

"I'd never lie to you, Tory."

"I never said you were, Bill. I'm sayin' it don't look like you're about to prospect for gold. More likely you're about to prospect for somebody who's found gold."

Bill Nunan squared his shoulders to me. He said, "Least-ways I ain't like his son, sittin' round the reservation while his pa fends for himself. Leastways I ain't thinkin' more about chasin' tail than I am my old man's . . ."

He started to duck but my fist opened his right eyebrow. I followed up with the left—my very best shot, flush on the jaw—but he took it standing up. He flung himself forward and grasped me by the collarbone and twisted me over onto the ground. I landed hard on my back and we rolled under the horses. All those legs and hooves churning in the dust made him let go and I sprung back, and when the horses skittered sidewise I charged into Bill's belly with my head down. That tumbled him over backwards, but as we landed he got a knee up and knocked the wind from out of me.

I reckon his six-shooter slipped from its holster when his

leg went up, for I landed on it. He was rising to his feet when I got the Colt in hand and cocked it. The sound froze him solid. I got my legs under me, ribs paining me fierce, the breath coming hard and my heart hammering, and I thought I might kill him. But I studied him then and saw the blood running into his eye, and I saw the hate and the fear plain on his face, and it come to me what a weak and piteous creature he was—and I become less eager for killing and more wishful just to be rid of him. He'd saved my skin back in that buffalo wallow, and I reckoned that sparing him now made us even. I let the hammer down and tossed the Colt in the dirt.

Wouldn't you know, he sprung for it like a cat. He got aholt of the pistol and before he even got upright again it was pointed my way. I was so took with the wonder of it that I don't think I flinched when he fired.

CHAPTER 10

WHEN I am dead I intend to ask the Lord why Bill's bullet did not kill me. An inch or two nearer my nose and it would have. Instead it just scored my cheek. To this day I shave careful on that place. The lead smarted some and the shock of it knocked me down—but in other respects I considered myself right fortunate.

The problem here was that Bill was by no means through. As I lay there Bill reared back and let loose another round. It blasted the ground alongside my head and filled my ear with sand. I knew the next would be on the fly directly, so I rolled to my right and scuttled for cover.

But he didn't shoot. Something took his mind off it. Another gun. The gunman was somewhere up above us— one of the boardinghouse windows. His shot hit the hitching rail and splintered it. Then he fired again—whoever it was— and the bullet thumped at the base of the storehouse clear across the street. The next one struck the big iron pulley dangling from the loft, and sang away.

One thing was plain. As a pistol shot, this feller that had come to my aid wasn't worth spit.

Me and Bill had attracted some spectators—a couple of the Greeley boys and various Ute layabouts. All concerned commenced to scatter now like so many partridges. Bill forgot all about killing me and rushed to untie the horses. He leapt on the bay and yanked its head around, and then three more shots come flying. One hit a sack of seed wheat on the back of a wagon across the way and the grain come spilling out. Another whapped the ground closer to Bill and the third struck amongst his horse's hooves. The beast reared back, liking none of it. But if nothing else, Bill Nunan could handle a horse—and he got this one straightened out and spurred him down the street, the packhorse in tow.

I'd hunkered down under all this shooting and was considerable relieved when it stopped. I'd followed the sound to the boardinghouse window and knew it was Uncle Noah sticking up for me—but an old right-handed feller bangin' away left-handed with a pistol—and after we'd shared more than one or two snorts together, well, I was glad to hear the silence return.

"You go with what you got," he said later, when I'd drug myself back up the stairs to our room. "Just take it for luck you left two ready pistols up here. I ain't figured it out yet so's I can load 'em one-handed."

I was lucky and I knew it. I said, "Can you savvy that— tryin' to kill me when I'd had the drop on him and . . ."

"What did you expect him to do, Tory boy? There's certain men need killin' the first time around."

That may of summed it up. But still and all, after I'd chewed it over, what Bill had said out there in the street had me thinking.

"You reckon what he said was true, Uncle? Am I doin' right by Pa?" I had a hard time looking him in the eye so I stared out the window. "We been ten days hereabouts. Maybe this Dutchman feller will get here and won't even know where Pa's at."

I turned back to him and his look was sober. "I think you're doin' right, son, or I would've told you previous to this."

"And there's no particle of truth in what he said—about Josie, I mean? That I'm thinking more about love than about Pa?"

"I recollect he said chasin' tail."

"He did."

He thought on it a good while before he spoke again. "I

think you may be in love, Tory. I don't think you're chasin' tail."

Well, this was a day for revelations. And it wasn't hardly over, as all at once there come a knock on the door and it was Josie.

Her eyes were real wide, looking me over. "They said you'd been shot."

I turned my cheek toward her and said that, as gunshots go, this here wasn't much to brag on.

"I looked for blood on the stairs," she said. "I was so scared."

She touched her fingertips to my face. I can say for a fact that I recall the feel of Josie's fingers as if she'd done it this morning. After a minute or two, Uncle Noah made some kind of skitterish sound and out he went.

Josie went over to the basin and poured some water. I watched her. She wore no bonnet this time, just her yellow hair pulled back on her head, her face as fresh as flowers. She come over and washed the dirt off my face, and after she got the crease in my cheek cleaned out I opened my shirt and let her study the purple blotch just below my heart where Bill had kneed me. She touched it. The breath still rasped in my lungs and I reckoned I had me a cracked rib or two. I also reckoned that if I didn't do it now I'd never do it, so I kissed her.

She pulled away. It seems like she was always pulling away. She straightened herself up and spoke like nothing had happened.

She said, "I met a German count in Denver who had a scar like the one you're going to have. It was very distinguished."

Far as I was concerned, it was just another to add to my collection. I said, "Think I'm distinguished?"

She shook her head. "No. Too young."

"How about gallant?"

"No. Too brash."

"Well, what am I, then?"

"What you are, Tory Bowhunter, is a rowdy young cowboy who's so full of himself sometimes I just want to hit you."

"You already done that once," I said. I moved to grab her wrists.

She dodged me and laughed pretty. "And I may have to again."

I tried to give chase, but between them ribs of mine and other sundry bruises I wasn't as spry as I might have wished.

"This ain't no way to treat a bung-up patient, Josie."

"Miss Meeker," she said.

"Well then," I said, "enough of this." I set down on the bed some distance from where she stood—which was fortunate for both of us as Josie's ma and pa showed in the doorway not ten seconds afterward.

Arvilla made quite a little fuss over me, and Josie, prim as could be, said that I was gonna live in spite of doing everything a man could do to get himself killed.

"What you need is to choose your companions with more care," Meeker said. "A young man builds his future on the foundation of solid acquaintances."

"That is a certainty," I said.

That night the Meekers had us to supper. It was just me and Noah and Meeker and Arvilla and Josie gathered around a long table in Meeker's dining room. It had a lacy tablecloth and gold-plated candlesticks and suchlike. We even got to use Arvilla's best china, which she told us her ma had passed on to her back in Ohio, when Arvilla was a sixteen-year-old girl and this handsome dry-goods salesman by the name of Meeker come through and swept her off her feet. Round the edge of each plate, there were two plump little angels in baby-blue nighties, blowing trumpets and streaming ribbons behind them. It was all right pretty.

Now out comes Jane. Arvilla's got her serving supper. We were having chicken. Seemed like since we'd got here we'd eaten a hundred chickens. Arvilla had cut this one into little chunks and mixed in a bunch of turnips and onions—but it was still chicken. I'd never much liked chicken, and as each day passed I was growing to like it less. Sitting there pushing the stuff around on my plate got me to thinking about Miller again—him somewheres up north in Wyoming hunting game under government contract. The fact that the Dutchman was late in returning explained the lack of red meat hereabouts. I asked Meeker why it was that he'd hired someone to bring game into the agency, when the Utes could hunt him up all the meat he'd ever want.

"I will not buy game from the Indians," he said. He laid down his knife and fork and pulled his napkin out of his collar. I begun to fear I was in for more of an explanation than I might have wanted. "The Ute economy, lad, is based on game." He leaned back and laid his hands on the arms of his chair. "The Ute produces life's every essential from the game he slaughters, and those things which are not essential—whiskey and repeating rifles, for example—he procures by killing game and trading the hides." He spoke slow, so's we wouldn't miss a thing. "This economy, however, requires unlimited freedom of movement. If the game is gone here, the Ute moves there." He shifted a couple of spoons around to illustrate. "But I must ask you, lad, what is to happen when the Indian finds his freedom circumscribed—or even eliminated?"

I said, "I reckon he'll just . . ."

"I'll tell you what will happen. He will have to learn the white man's economy—farm the land, raise his own livestock, learn the value of a dollar—or he will perish."

"Seems like he might make an honest dollar if you was to buy the game off him," I said. I was irked. Principle is one thing—what you eat is another.

"It's not an honest dollar he's after," Arvilla said.

Meeker halted in the middle of chewing his food. "What's that, Mother?"

Arvilla looked unsure. It seemed maybe she wished to take

the words back. But others jumped out—she'd held them in too long. "He—all of them, Nathan—they want you to work and for them to play. You've worked yourself half to death here. You'll probably die on this farm, die trying to save them, and all they'll ever feel for you is . . ."

"Hate." Josie said it. It come out real soft, like a thought.

There followed a good deal of silence. I wondered if Meeker's wife and daughter had ever before let him know what they thought. But when the old man spoke now, he sounded casual-like, almost cheery.

He said, "I think you'll be happy to hear what I told Douglas today. It's time he and his people understood just where flour comes from."

It got real silent now. No one even chewed.

"Flour comes from wheat," he said. "Wheat comes from the earth—which you must first plow, and then seed. Beginning tomorrow, Shadrach will plow the two hundred acres just south of Douglas's lodges."

Josie said, "That's pony pasture."

Meeker said, "Beginning tomorrow, it will be planted in winter wheat."

"Will you leave them the racetrack?" Josie asked.

Meeker shook his head—just once. Then dug in for more supper. "Mother, your biscuits are extraordinary."

Noah said, "Meeker, you're the dumbest man I ever met."

"I beg your pardon?"

"You're dumb, Meeker. Dumb as a melon rind. You reckon you're gonna show the Utes who's boss, right? Once and for all?"

Meeker come as close as he could to a sly smile. "That's right."

"They'll kill you."

The smile stayed right there. "They won't, because they'll starve. I've let them know that if they disagree too strongly, I'll withhold their annuity goods."

So that explained the big powwow at Douglas's encampment during the afternoon. Meeker had made a threat, and the chiefs had to talk it over.

"Is that your hole card?" Noah said.

Meeker let the question hang there for a space. "I haven't shown my hole card, Mr. Bowhunter. The fact is, I have about two hundred hole cards at Ft. Fred Steele, near Rawlins, Wyoming."

Josie let out a gasp.

"The Indians call them long knives," Meeker said.

I slept uneasy that night and when the rifle shot woke me I thought I might be dreaming. I peered out the window, past Josie's schoolhouse and the log outbuildings and the livestock pens. It would soon be daybreak, the hills just starting to lighten but the valley still dark and chilly. I heard another shot.

Noah was beside me.

"A carbine, I make it. Yonder by the river."

Our eyes moved over the pasture. No sound for the longest time, just the fog thinning over the grass. We could just make out the Indian ponies stirring at the smell of daybreak.

And then here come Shadrach Price, his legs hard pressed to keep up with the rest of him. There was blood all over his face. I had my gun out from under the bed and I was down the stairs by the time he reached the front porch.

The Greeley boys all rushed down in their nightgowns to meet him, but Shad said, "Wait, I gotta tell Mr. Meeker." He breathed hard. There was plenty of blood but it was a cut on his brow and nothing more.

Now the old man got there. He'd took the time to pull on his britches and his coat before coming out in the street. "No cause for alarm, lads. Let's hear what Shad has to say."

"They shot at me, sir. I thought I'd get an early start on the plowing, and they shot at me."

"*At* you, lad?"

"I reckon so, sir, but they clean missed. The team took off

with the plow and drug me a ways. Cut my head on the blade."

"Ah," Meeker said. "Then it was a warning shot." A little smile crept onto his face. "So I thought."

I said, "Mr. Meeker, you tellin' us their bark is worse than their bite?"

"I might have expressed it differently, lad, but yes. But the Utes have erred seriously in discharging their weapons. They are now clearly in the wrong."

"Beggin' your pardon, Mr. Meeker, but—matters of right and wrong aside—the Indians are firing guns around here."

He looked at me with that way he had, so patient and reasonable-like that I wanted to kill him. "I can appreciate your concern, lad. But you've got to know your enemy. We're in no danger."

I wasn't gonna press matters. He heard only what he wanted to hear, anyway.

"Thompson, Hickett, please stay behind," Meeker said. "The rest of you—why don't you get some breakfast. Everything will be all right. That is a certainty."

We were turning the corner of the boardinghouse to go in by the side door. Noah said to me, kind of low, "You notice something different in the way he talked?"

"I know I didn't like it none."

"More'n that. He said you got to know your enemy."

"Enemy?"

He nodded and smiled, his eyes sharp. "That's how I heard it. Kind of a new twist, wouldn't you say?"

Shadrach was a hero at the breakfast table. Josie bandaged up his head. His young'uns set one on either leg, and his wife Flora Ellen wrapped herself around his shoulders.

Jane fetched out the grub about as quick as she ever had, and most of the boys were cheerful and excited, like to be shot at was an adventure. I'd been shot at before and didn't find it so exciting. Neither did Noah. He was finally fit enough to come to breakfast for the first time since we'd arrived at White River. Last time he was at this here table, he was laying on it.

After we ate, Josie led me and Noah outside where the cordwood was piled. It was full daylight now, a fine clear September morning just like any other—except there were no Utes about.

"They ought to be here soon enough," Josie said. "Monday is the day they pick up the week's annuity goods at the storehouse."

"Still and all," I said, "you wonder 'bout the rest of 'em."

Breakfast broke up inside and the boys moved past us on their way to work. Thompson and Hickett stopped alongside us. Thompson hemmed and hawed, I guess on account of Josie being there.

"Tory, you know there's trouble shapin' here," Thompson said.

"Maybe," I said.

Hickett said, "You know there is."

"Listen, Tory," Thompson said. "The old man says we're not to release any flour to the Indians today. Not flour nor cornmeal nor nothin' else."

Noah whistled two little notes.

I said, "What are you supposed to tell 'em?"

Thompson's Adam's apple moved up and down. "Nothing, I guess. Just send 'em over to the agent's office. The old man—sorry, ma'am—Mr. Meeker says he wants to share some thoughts with Douglas."

I was thinking he'd better share some of that flour, too, else there'd be hell to pay.

"What should we do?" Hickett said.

"I reckon you do what he says."

"You gonna be close at hand?"

"Reckon so."

They moved on. Me and Josie and Noah stood there. Noah said, "This about your pa, ma'am?"

Josie let out a sigh that was almost the start of tears. "So much is happening. I just . . ."

I didn't need to hear more. I just looked down at the ground. I wanted to hold her. I knew, though, that holding wasn't what Josie needed, for she wasn't one to hide away safe from a troublesome thing, but to face up to it. I guess Noah had a feel for it, too, for he just hung fire then as I did, and waited on her to speak.

"My father won't talk." Her eyes moved back and forth between us. "You have to understand, he always talks. Especially to me. Thinking and dreaming and telling you what it is he's thought up—that's my father's way. It's what he's done his whole life—dreaming things and talking other folks into dreaming along with him."

That rung true enough. He'd had a dream for these Utes. He'd spent a year and a half trying to make them swallow it. But they'd just coughed it back in his face.

Noah said, "Injuns got dreams of their own, Miss Meeker."

Josie shook her head. "He's changed so. It's like he has to punish them." She looked up at us, her eyes crowded with pain and love and anger. "I'm so helpless."

Noah touched her shoulder with his hand. "A man's pride can be a load to carry, Miss Josie. But you can't carry it for him."

Something drew my attention. Down the street, from the west side, four Utes come ahorseback.

Douglas led, and left to right in his wake it was Colorow, Antelope, and Douglas's son Loud Cry. They come at a walk—all business they were—the four of them fit to strike awe in your heart. These weren't reservation Indians no longer. Chief Douglas stepped his white horse stately and slow, his gaze almost kingly, a great patterned breastplate of malachite and hammered silver on his chest. Behind him even Colorow had an air, and alongside Colorow there was Antelope, wearing nothing on his chest but an open buckskin vest, his arms bare and muscled. Him and Loud Cry carried carbines in their left hand. Loud Cry's pony snorted. The sun struck them all in the face. They looked straight into it—and though you knew they saw everything, they looked like they weren't looking at nothing. It was like they weren't just Indians, but some different sort of creature. Something secret.

They drew rein before the storehouse.

Half an hour later we were in Meeker's office, the room well nigh full of Utes. They'd told the boys at the storehouse that they'd just help themselves to what was due them. And they had. Now Nathan Meeker set behind his desk, casual-like, and Douglas strode up to it. Josie stood at her pa's back, me and Noah off to the side. Around the front wall of the office, by the door to the hallway, the three other braves formed a picket line.

For some reason I noticed the little things. I saw the vein running along the muscle of Antelope's arm. I looked down at the Indians' moccasins and thought about the work shoes they wouldn't wear. I smelled the oil in their hair. And then as Meeker got to his feet, I saw him on one side of the desk and Douglas on the other, both of them tall and straight and gray-haired and proud and fixed in their place. One in his broadcloth, one in his buckskins, each staring at the other with their sharp eyes from the far sides of creation.

Douglas said, "To take what belongs to us is not to steal." The chief wasn't pleading no case. He was stating the truth as he saw it, just to be understood.

"There is no voucher for the goods, Douglas. If you take them, it will be seen as thievery. Punishable as thievery." His gaze held with Douglas's for a spell, then dropped to his desk. He begun to shuffle papers around. "It is your choice."

Douglas kept the mask on. His face told you nothing, but his eyes were quick and bright. He studied the old man and read him, and when he spoke he got to the core of the matter. "Meeker not here to punish the Utes."

I looked at Josie. The color run out of her face. That word "punish"—she'd spoke the same word to us outside. She was close to these Indians. Somewhere up the line she'd talked it over with them, maybe given them sympathy, even counsel.

Meeker's eyes snapped up from his papers. "Punishment has nothing to do with it. This will be much-needed discipline."

The chief said, "Meeker forgets. Indian agent is sent to work for the Indians."

"I work for your welfare as I see it. You must learn that things will not always be given to you."

The mask slipped just for a moment, just a flicker. There was anger behind it, and something like great sadness. "Utes trade land for these goods. Goods belong to us."

Meeker held firm. "The treaty you refer to has many provisions," he said. "One is that you will be peaceable. I don't know what your people have been doing when off this reservation. I've heard of vast destruction brought about by fire. But while on this reservation you will not make trouble. You will not raise arms against the white man. This morning you did."

"You give much cause."

Meeker's voice rose fast. All the fury the old man had hid began to rush forth. "You will not intimidate me!" And then as quickly as it showed its face, it hid again. Meeker's hands gripped the edge of the desk so hard his fingernails went white. "Beginning in a day or two, my workers will begin to string barbed wire once again. They will also resume plowing where you have raced your horses. Thereafter, you will tend the crops. You will need to grow wheat if you intend to make bread."

"To do these things will starve my horses."

Meeker gave him his gaze direct and cold. "No need for them to suffer. We'll pare the herd down as mercifully as possible. Say, fifty to begin with."

Loud Cry covered the room in three steps and leapt for

the old man's throat. The Indian's war cry froze me where I stood. Loud Cry cleared the desk and drove Meeker into the wall, the old man's chair scraping backwards and tangling up his feet and those of the Indian so that they both went down. Josie got knocked off to the side and screamed "Father!" and Loud Cry got his hands around Meeker's throat and pulled him to his feet just as I yanked my Colt and thumbed the hammer back. At the sound of it, Loud Cry looked over his shoulder at me as if he might let up, but then I heard Noah yell, "Tory!" and from the corner of my eye I saw the barrel of Antelope's carbine swing level with my chest.

In that instant it was mine to decide. Turn and shoot Antelope, or drop Loud Cry first and turn after. Or maybe, just maybe, let the moment pass. At this range Antelope's .44 Spencer would blow me against the wall by the time I turned on him. Maybe he wasn't yet ready to kill a white man. Maybe none of us was ready to kill. But how did you know?

We were on the wire edge, the lot of us.

Instinct decides these things. There wasn't the time for pondering. Maybe a month previous I'd have blasted away. But I wasn't ten feet distant now from the girl I cared for, and I had my one-armed uncle beside me with his gun still in his belt. There was Josie's poor old pa with Loud Cry's thumbs on his throat—that foolish old man who lugged his pride around like the cross. What I had now was connections—connections to people—and I reckon the feeling of connections just seeped through me and stayed my hand.

All I could hear was Antelope breathing hard. All I could feel was my body coiled, every hair alive, waiting.

And then Josie screamed, "Nicaagat!"

He stood in the door, Sowerwick at his back.

He said, "Raise your guns."

If by that he meant just me, I was first going to shoot him dead. But he waved a hand at Antelope, and though Antelope was Douglas's man, I don't reckon any Ute would have argued with Jack. Not at that moment, not with the look in Jack's eye.

Sowerwick carried a carbine—same make as Antelope's—but his boss strode into the room empty-handed. He sported fringed buckskins again, a long-handled knife in the sash about his waist. That was all he bore in the way of arms, but it made its impression on you. He greeted Douglas real solemn-like, and then he told Loud Cry to let Meeker go. Loud Cry let him drop like a sack of flour.

Josie knelt to help her pa, but Jack said, "Leave us. Him not hurt bad." When she didn't move, his voice grew just a shade softer. "Go."

"You won't hurt him."

"No."

Josie touched the old man's head where it had banged the wall. She stood up and flattened her dress against her legs. Her glance flickered over my way—here and gone too quick for me to read it—and she hurried past Jack.

Jane was in the doorway. Past Josie's back I could see the look of gloating in the Indian girl's eyes, and I knew the two women were seeing deep into each other, and then Josie pushed by her.

Noah caught my eye. If Jack had lied just now, and meant to do harm to Josie's pa and the rest of us, there wasn't much that me and my uncle could do but take a Ute or two with us when we died. It would be Jack first, Douglas next. I had a yen for Colorow but there wouldn't be time. A smile crinkled Noah's eyes, and I couldn't help but smile myself. It wasn't much, but if a good-bye was needed, it would do.

I had the notion, though, that Jack hadn't lied. Some version of Indian honor come into play where Josie was concerned. I guess Jack had himself some wounded pride to work off—it hadn't been twenty-four hours since I'd showed him up on the racetrack—so pride might have required him to show her he was tough. But I didn't expect he'd go back on his word once he give it to her.

Now Josie's pa gathered himself up and the stubborn light rekindled in his eyes. He dusted his chest with the palms of his hands and run his fingers up through his hair. He set his jaw again and stared into Loud Cry's eyes.

"This will not go unpunished," Meeker said.

Now I thought Jack might hit him. The Indian's body revolved to the right like he might bring a fist back around. Meeker sensed it and flinched. But then Jack caught himself, and through clenched teeth he hissed out his words.

"You will punish no one."

It was Douglas's son that Meeker had threatened, and now it was Douglas that spoke to the old man. "Your time is done. You will leave here with your high talk. Let your White Father send another agent."

By now that would have been all right with me. I was tallying up the numbers here at the agency—eleven white men, three white women, two white young'uns. Counting Douglas's band and Jack's band, we faced maybe seven hundred Utes.

Judging by his silence, I thought that old Meeker, too, may well have known it was time to go. I thought I read relief in his face—as if Douglas's telling him to quit White River might be an honest way out.

But then Jack said, "It is too late for that."

CHAPTER 11

DOUGLAS'S head turned slow, those sharp eyes of his fixed on Jack. He asked a question without speaking a word. Jack looked back at him steady, making him wait on the answer—for he surely wished Douglas to chew for a spell on the fact that he'd got the word and Douglas hadn't.

Finally Jack said, "Soldiers come."

I looked past him to Meeker. It was true. He'd done it. I saw him sag through the shoulders. His hole card had just fell to the floor, face up.

Jack said, "My scouts ride far on the Agency Road, I have spoken with them. Two hundred long knives. Horses and many guns."

Douglas's eyes narrowed. Plain to say, this was the first he'd heard of this. Still, he was chief, and if there was surprise or anger or fear inside him, he hid it. He murmured quietly to Jack in Ute, cool and business-like. He'd been chief for some time and he knew how it was done.

Jack answered in English. "Three days ride for them."

Colorow came forward and passed a few words in Ute with Douglas. Loud Cry made his feelings known, too, and by the tone of it I thought it best to let my hand ease down to my pistol. I stepped a hair back of the stovepipe so's Antelope might not see it—but Sowerick caught sight of the motion and lifted his carbine. Noah's hand moved just a trace toward his Colt. Jack twisted round to see, the fingers of his right hand curling about the long bone handle of his knife.

All this was sudden and silent, like so many cats moving in the dark. But it was a standoff again. The Utes had the numbers, but they weren't ready to make their play. Not yet.

Meeker said, "It was to prevent just this sort of belligerence that I sent for the cavalry several days ago."

We all turned to him. His was courage that came and went—a cowardly man trying to be strong, or else a strong man whose string had finally broke. You couldn't rightly tell. "Should you do us harm, you will call them down upon yourselves."

Douglas spoke in reply. "Many time Meeker call himself friend. Many time we talk, and Meeker say, 'Open your heart, Douglas. Hear my words.' Now I hear, Meeker. Your soldiers speak plenty."

"Douglas," he said, plaintive again, "I *am* your friend."

"Speak no more of this."

"I am your friend. The soldiers come for your own good. They will keep the young firebrands under control. All the good works you and I have done—all the good works yet to do—they will not be put to waste."

"No," Douglas said. "Indians hear these words before. My people not die like sheep. Meeker does not remember Sand Creek. Meeker does not remember Washita. Not like Indian remembers."

"But I do! That is why we must pull together, you and I, to prevent this tragic . . ."

Jack said, "Enough talk. The long knives will go back."

The old man sighed heavy. "That is impossible, Nicaagat. It's true I sent for them, but they would not have left Ft. Steele without orders from their superiors. I cannot revoke those orders myself."

Once again the Utes spoke amongst themselves. There was some dispute going on. The young ones grew hot, but Douglas raised an open hand and quieted them. Then he spoke to Meeker once again.

"You will keep the soldiers away." He poked a thumb in my direction. "You send boy to tell them. Him bring chief of long knives here. We talk. Only one soldier come onto Ute land."

Jack said, "More come, much killing." The others murmured around him, sounding like they were all for that. Douglas was wise enough to know where their feelings were headed—towards Jack and away from him. He said to the agent, "Meeker, do not bring on trouble."

The old man pushed out his jaw one more time, and said, "Don't threaten me."

And then Douglas said, more sorrowful than anything else, "You are a fool."

"You comin' along?"

"Thought I might."

"That's good, Uncle. We might as well both get killed as one."

"Won't happen," Noah said. "The Utes want us to get through. They'll be watchin' sure enough, but they won't make trouble." He grinned. " 'Course, comin' back might be different."

"Well, I'll be comin' back." I was thinking of Meeker's daughter.

"Listen, Tory. Could be Josie ought to come along. Then neither of us would have to come back."

"I been thinkin' on it. I don't think she'll leave her folks."

"Go ask her. I'll wait on you."

Josie come into the parlor, brushing a stray hair from her cheek. Her eyes were bright with tears.

"Father told me what happened."

"Is he here now?"

"Yes."

I looked hard but I couldn't read her. I'll confess that with all that was going on, my thoughts still dwelt on the way she looked, and on things like the bare part of her neck where her collar stopped. I was learning something—that it is a powerful tide a young man runs with.

"Will you come out on the porch with me?"

We set out there, the two of us gazing straight ahead. Her house marked the end of Josie's Lane. There was nothing across from it save pasture made green by her father's Grand Canal. Yonder the Danforth Hills stood pale and dotted with sagebrush, lit sharp from the east, white clouds blowing toward us out of the north. Strawberry Creek flowed through the foothills, just a trickle now, the willows along its banks still as green as summer.

"Be a late fall," I said.

The wind roused some of the dust in the street. I thought, this is all gonna blow away.

"I talked with them," Josie said. "Talked with Douglas, tried to make him see." She looked right at me now. "Tory, it's just that nobody understands anybody else. They talk but nothing happens. Douglas doesn't understand my father, Father doesn't understand him or his people." Her eyes looked so straight into mine, I could feel them. "And now cavalry."

I said, "Did you tell Jack they was comin'?"

"I didn't even know. Not till today."

"But he sent out scouts. Someone must have told him."

"It was Jane." For the first time she started to cry. "I thought I knew her. Nobody knows anybody around here."

I set there beginning to savvy what it was that drew me to her. She was a rare thing, Josie Meeker. She took the feelings of other folks into her heart—the way those hummingbirds of hers took nectar. But she was just a woman, and when her own heart was full she needed someone to share it with— and she had nobody. I reckon any young man who set at Josie's side as she wept, and who had kissed her the previous day, would have thought himself just the one.

"You come with us," I said, "me and Noah. It'll be sunup tomorrow by the time we reach the troops. We'll tell 'em what we've got to tell 'em, and then we'll keep going."

She just smiled my way and shook her head.

"The odds are bad here," I said.

"I can't leave Mother."

"Bring her."

"She won't leave my father. And he won't leave his work. We already asked him."

I knew that, even if he'd been amind to, Meeker couldn't have said yes. He was a hostage. They were all hostages. That's what Noah and I hadn't said to each other in the stable just now—but we both knew it. That was why I'd come to see Josie.

But maybe there was more driving me. Maybe I just needed to know if, given the chance, she'd choose to go with me.

Our time was running short. I tried to say something hopeful. "It'll be all right. Your pa says the commanding officer's a feller name of Thornburgh. I'll ride back with him. Can't tell, Josie—things as they are, could be you're safer here than on the Agency Road."

"The Indians won't harm me," she said, like that was the least of her worries. "Nicaagat wouldn't let them."

I looked at her as filled with wonder as I've ever been. "You said no one really knows no one else around here. What makes you so sure of Jack?"

She looked away, and I wished bitterly in my heart that she hadn't smiled.

"A woman knows."

Me and Noah rode out the way we'd come in, east-by-northeast, tracing the meander of White River back to higher ground. We passed through two miles or so of what they called The Narrows, where Powell Park got squeezed between the Danforth Hills to the north and the bare jutty rocks of the Grand Hogback to the south. The grass thinned out to sand and blue sage, and the hills above us showed piñon and cedar.

By noon we'd covered ten or twelve miles taken together. On the bench above the river, we found the signs of Jack's lodges—but sign is all we found. They'd picked up and left.

There wasn't much in the way of lodges or rope pens for the horses or anything else—just plenty of chewed-up ground. The tracks were fresh. Judging by the ruts left by their travois poles, we reckoned the squaws and their young'uns and the old folks were on their way south over Roan Plateau, tôward Grand River country. The fighting men, the braves, they'd posted north, up the Agency Road.

"Goin' to greet the cavalry," I said.

Noah said, "That's a way of puttin' it."

We made sure the horses were watered well, and then we turned up the Agency Road. It hadn't changed much since last we'd rode that way—still dusty and rutted and rock-strewn, the ground all about it marked by shallow gulches and dry streambeds.

Directly the canyon walls rose up fast, until the western side of the canyon, and then the road itself, and then the base of the rocky wall on the right, all fell into shadow. The canyon narrowed and cover was scant. I thought, if old Major Thornburgh decides to bring his column through Coal Creek Canyon, this part will be slippery going.

It was for Noah and me to keep the major out of here— leastways to tell him what the deal was so he could make a choice. This here stretch was called Yellowjacket Pass. It lacked six or eight miles to the reservation line at Milk Creek. North of that line the soldiers might camp unmolested. Cross it, Douglas had said, and his braves would make war.

We come down out of the pass into broken country. The Agency Road crossed the same gravelly creek bed twice or three times in the space of five miles. There was plenty of sun now that the steep canyon walls were behind us. But still there was rimrock to either side, with a wide shelf laying just under the rim to the left where any number might hide. On our right the wall stood nearer the road and not so tall, but the land fell away sharp behind the rim so that a man might lay there unseen and keep close watch on the road.

A mile or two further and the road bent round to the

right. The valley swung open to the north and west. We set our horses, gazing for a spell at the tall sandstone hills on the yon side. Down below us the basin was a quarter-mile across, but grew wider as your eyes moved north. Plenty of short grass hereabouts, though browned off for lack of rain, and clumps of rabbit brush with blossoms a bright yellow. The creek that had cut this valley was no more'n ten feet across but with banks as tall as a man's shoulder. The water stood in pools here and there, and what there was of it had a chalky color—like somebody upstream had spilt a bucketful of milk.

It had taken us nigh unto four hours to come this far, pushing the horses some but knowing that we'd feel a mite better once we got north of Milk Creek. We still had rimrock at our back. Up ahead, a day's ride or thereabouts, Major Thornburgh and his cavalry train were wending their way south.

I fetched forth two strips of jerky and offered Noah one. Before I bit into mine, I held it up to the ridge overhead and called out, "How 'bout some supper?" But there were no takers.

By midnight we'd fifteen more miles behind us. We found a draw where to make camp. A little spring come trickling out from amongst the rocks and you could see the moonlight in it. I got to thinking there, standing by Temper and petting his neck as he drank, and not watching like I should have. A loud halloo come ringing from just past the trees. I jumped like I'd been poked in the rump.

The stranger told us who he was and what he was up to, and we let him draw close.

He said, "Nervous, boy?"

The light was good enough to see him. He was fat and moved slow, and he led a horse with knock-knees. His name was Charlie Wheelwright, and it turns out he was Major Thornburgh's scout. By the looks of him, he'd never been nervous a day in his life. This here was a laughing man—fact, I reckon he'd been drinking—and he talked a whole lot louder than you'd expect of a scout on a bright night.

We lowered our guns. "Just edgy," I said. "There'd be Indians about."

He grinned. "That would be understatin' it."

"Then you know?"

"Why sure, son. That's what scouts are for. Indians all over—thick as fleas. What is it brings you boys this way?"

I told him we were carrying word from White River, a message for Major Thornburgh.

"That right?" Wheelwright said. "Carryin' word myself—for the agent down there." He swept his hat off his head and took a bow. It was a right nice hat—sort of sandy-colored, with the tallest crown I ever saw. Turned out that underneath it Charlie Wheelwright was as bald as an egg. "Major Thornburgh," he said, "wishes to inform Mr. Meeker of his imminent arrival."

I said, "If Major Thornburgh arrives too imminent, Major Thornburgh will arrive dead."

Noah said, "The Utes are layin' for your major somewheres south of Milk Creek."

"That right?" He thought it over. "Best to tell him."

Noah said, "You ever been through Coal Creek Canyon?"

"Once or twice."

"Then you gotta reckon it this way." He explained it real careful-like, for plain to say this Wheelwright feller was none too sharp. Noah said that if you had yourself a hundred Indians up on those canyon walls, you could just about massacre two or three times that many soldiers on the road below.

He asked the scout just how many men rode with Thornburgh.

He smoothed his whiskers with his fingertips. "Well, I dunno," he said. "Might be a hundred eighty, thereabouts.

'Long with three hundred fifty horses. Supply train—twenty wagons, maybe."

We'd already calculated the number of Indians the major might expect. Jack's force would number forty or forty-five braves—all of them on the muscle or they wouldn't be running with Jack in the first place. By now Douglas's bunch would be with them. That would bring it to a hundred twenty braves—maybe a hundred twenty-five taken together.

Me and Noah had been there with Meeker when he wrote the note for Thornburgh. We told Wheelwright what was in it. The old man and Douglas and Jack had agreed that Thornburgh would camp his force somewhere to the north of Milk Creek, and then travel on to White River. He could take no more'n five men with him. Once he got there, him and Meeker and the Ute muckety-mucks would sit down together and sort things out. Right now the Indians' apprehensions were running high—that's the way Meeker put things—and though an Indian agent couldn't countermand the major's orders, he hoped the major would see that this new course of action was in the best interests of all concerned.

"Reasonable enough," Wheelwright said, looking serious like a lawyer. "Leastways, to you and me." Directly he reached inside his belt and fetched forth a bottle. " 'Course, we ain't soldiers."

Noah said, "No offense, Charlie, but how long you been a cavalry scout?"

Wheelwright pulled the cork with his teeth. "Thursday last."

I said, "What's your regular line of work?"

"Ain't got a regular line of work," he said, kinda mumbly what with the cork still in his mouth.

I glanced over at Uncle. He asked old Charlie how far up the trail the major's camp might be.

"Oh, I dunno. Near to a mile, maybe." He took a belt and held out the bottle. "Just left there, myself."

Noah's jaw kind of dropped a fraction. If the cavalry was just a mile distant, what in hell were we doing here talking to this drunk? But Noah just laughed and took what was offered.

It was well nigh one o'clock in the morning when we got past the picket line and roused the major, but he come out of his tent alert and cheerful and had his orderly bring us coffee. In the campfire light b had an honest, smooth-shaven face. By my reckoning he wasn't yet thirty-five. He had an easterner's way of talking and small knowledge of the country, but he didn't pretend otherwise.

"My first concern, gentlemen, is the safety of this command," he said. "Secondly, that of the people at the White River Agency. Do you gentlemen feel it possible that Mr. Meeker wrote this message under duress?"

Noah scowled. "You mean does he want you to do what he says he wants you to do?"

"Yes."

"Well, I'd say so," Noah said, kind of irritated. "A man couldn't make it much plainer."

The major took no offense. "All I've got to go on, Mr. Bowhunter, is what's here on paper—along with anything you and your nephew can tell me of the situation firsthand. A man will write most anything with a knife at his throat."

"By my lights you couldn't make White River with this force if you wanted to. Not without bloodshed."

Thornburgh had an adjutant with him by the name of Sensibaugh, a lieutenant. This one didn't shave yet. He said, "If you're saying the threat of those Indians will dictate our course of action, you don't know the Third Cavalry."

Noah wrapped the fingers of his one hand round his coffee cup. The night had growed chilly and the steam rose before his face. He said, "That's pride talkin'. Pride's killed plenty men."

Charlie Wheelwright said he'd known a considerable number of Utes and not one would stand and fight if shots were fired.

I said, "Goin' on three weeks ago we were in a little mining town east of Hahn's Peak, called Tourmaline. Plenty of shots were fired, far as we could tell. When we got there all the white folks were dead."

That took some of the cheer out of old Charlie. "Utes?"

Noah answered him. "Appeared so."

Sensibaugh said, "Off the beaten track, wouldn't you say?"

"Maybe."

"That proves my point. Those people wouldn't have been killed if the army had been nearby."

The major got up from the fire and said, "We've got a couple of hours left to us to sleep on this. In any event I want to make the Milk Creek line by the afternoon." He asked if me and Uncle would ride point with him and the lieutenant come morning, and then he turned to Sensibaugh.

"Lieutenant, wake the men at four."

I crawled under the sutler's wagon and drug my saddle along for a pillow. But I couldn't sleep. Thinking of Josie done it. Forty miles lay between us. How many Utes was it guarded her and the rest? It'd be Douglas and his bunch. Colorow would be with them. And Loud Cry? I wondered if he'd gone up the canyon or hung back to keep the watch. My guess was that he'd want to linger at White River. That way, if word come down the Agency Road that fighting had broke out, he'd get to kill hostages. Loud Cry would like that.

As for the other Utes at White River, I doubted they were sure just what to do with Nathan Meeker. Like as not, all they could be certain of was that they had him. Maybe they figured it was all they needed. In my mind's eye I could see the Indians, hardly talking at all, just fingering their weapons, waiting on some rider to arrive with word from up the canyon—wondering all the time just how far this was gonna go.

I slithered out from beneath the wagon and walked over by where the horses were tied. I spent a while with Temper, brushing the dust out of his coat. He nickered softly, but otherwise there was no sound but for an owl or two—and I couldn't be sure if they were real owls or Indian owls. Owls never do make you feel real comfortable, anyway. I put my hand on Temper's neck.

"I'm glad to have you around," I said, feeling foolish for talking like that to a horse.

Before too long Lieutenant Sensibaugh woke the outfit. We were gone from there by first light—rumbling down off the divide and into Milk Creek Valley before the sun was an hour high. The major wrote out another message for Charlie Wheelwright to carry to White River. It said the major would take Meeker's suggestion under advisement and would more than likely fort up at Milk Creek for a spell and send word on from there.

Now with Charlie gone, me and Uncle were the only fellers on the expedition who'd seen the country. It was rousing for a young man to be caught up in such a thing—a hundred fifty blue-coated soldiers, wagons and animals in train behind them, with all their jangling of hardware and the creak of springs and wagon wheels. There was the dust trailing off their horses' hooves, the call of orders down the line, and at the head of the column a handsome young major who looks like he might make a senator some day, and who turns your way in the saddle and says, "Well, Bowhunter, what do you think?"

"Me, sir? How do you mean?"

"This bind we're in, son. You and your uncle here have brought me a dilemma to wrestle with. I wondered if you could help me out of it."

The major said that by his lights the Utes held one high card—their hostages. Thornburgh held one high card—his soldiers. To leave his command camped twenty-five miles from White River, and then go in alone, or practically alone, was to toss his high card on the pile, and for nothing.

"Besides," he said. "I might end up just one more hostage myself. That wouldn't do Nathan Meeker much good." He laughed. "Make me look pretty foolish, too."

"Well, sir," I said, "your other choice don't look that much better." I was growing a mite nervous that the major might make a run for it through Coal Creek Canyon.

"The only other choice, Bowhunter, at least as you've laid it out for me, would be to engage the enemy on his ground. And by what you say, I wouldn't get very many of this command through that canyon in one piece. The hostages would be killed before we got through, anyway. That smacks of failure to me, Bowhunter." He looked at me then, squinting hard in the sun, and I could see where the steel was in him. "This mission will not fail."

We ate in the saddle—hardtack and canteen water—and by late in the afternoon we'd drawn close to the reservation line. Milk Creek Valley begun to narrow, and we snaked along with the creek on our left and the banded hills squeezing in on the right. The major grew quiet. The wind kicked up the dust and some of us wore our bandannas. I watched the rim across the valley but saw nothing.

Then the major drew rein and held up his hand. We dismounted and let the horses graze. I reckoned it might take a quarter-hour for the column to bunch up behind us. While that happened, the major and Sensibaugh and me and Noah and two of the officers got down on our haunches to talk.

The major spoke slow and steady, just the way he'd thought it out. "Gentlemen," he said, "we're going to put a quick end to this business. An Indian cannot hold a gun to the head of the U.S. government. The longer we wait, the more likely it is they'll catch the scent of weakness in us, and once they do they'll never let the agency people go without a fight. So here's how I see it."

He held a stick in his hand, and as he laid out each point he made a scratch in the sand. "At this moment Douglas is unimportant. Nicaagat controls the warriors, therefore Nicaagat is the one for me to deal with. The question is not whether or not to negotiate, but where. I see no reason to do that some twenty-five miles from my command. The Milk Creek line makes more sense. We'll meet there, Nicaagat and me. I'll assure him that we mean no harm to him or his people. He'll believe me, gentlemen, because it is the truth.

"Then we'll ride in together—his forces and ours. Once this command is encamped at White River, the hostages will no longer be at risk. Then—and only then—having made our good will very plain, we'll be able to sit down—Meeker, the chiefs and I—and negotiate a peaceful resolution to the larger problems."

When his last point was made, he run a long scratch through all the others. He was a clever feller, Major Thornburgh was. He'd asked his questions, listened long and hard, and reasoned it through. We'd given him two choices. He didn't like either one, so he made up a third. Now he looked pleased and confident. Everything was gonna work out all right.

Noah said, "I got a question."

Major Thornburgh turned in his direction.

"Just how are you gonna get Jack to come out and powwow with you at the Milk Creek line?"

"Easy." Thornburgh grinned. "I'm going to cross it."

CHAPTER 12

LIEUTENANT Sensibaugh got the column formed up—save for the mule-drawn wagons that lagged half a mile behind us. We ventured the last mile at a slow walk, not saying much, just watchful. It wasn't late in the day, but the hills on our right were steep and the sun had slipped behind them. Along their base the wind had driven the sand into dunes of thirty feet or more. There was no getting a view up above them except by moving out a ways from the hills. We couldn't do that till we crossed Milk Creek, which run hard by us on our left.

On the yon side of the creek lay the better part of the valley—three hundred yards of grass and rabbit brush and white and blue wildflowers. Then the terrain grew bare and rose much like a flight of steps to the road where me and Noah had looked down on all this the day before. Above the road the rocky wall kind of glowered at you. Back of that there was nothing to see but blue sky.

I thought about what a pretty day this here was, how we were cluttering it up with troubles. I would have liked to be back at White River, chasing hummingbirds with Nathan Meeker's yellow-haired daughter.

Major Thornburgh didn't hesitate none. When we found a good fording place on Milk Creek, we just skittered down the banks and splashed across.

I looked back at the sand dunes. There was nothing to be seen. The sunlight was sharp along the ridge above them. Charlie Wheelwright had told the major there would be no trouble in Milk Creek Valley. He said the place for an ambush was Yellowjacket Pass, six or eight miles down the trail. The walls were steeper there, the cover was better, and the troops would be squeezing through a narrow canyon where they couldn't form up if they had to.

"Looks like our scout was right," the major said. "Be certain of one thing, though—they're watching us. We'll move slow, give them a chance to show themselves."

Sensibaugh made the point that the animals could use a good watering, and that Milk Creek wasn't the best place to do it. There wasn't all that much water in the creek bed, and what there was looked sour.

"Where is there good water?" the major asked.

"Beaver Springs," Uncle Noah said. "But that'd take us five miles inside the line."

"It's short of the pass, though?"

"Not far short."

Sensibaugh said, "We can't stay here indefinitely, sir. If we're to make camp tonight, we'll need better water than this."

The major chewed it over. He'd already cut his plans and didn't look too eager to make a change. But directly he said, "All right, Lieutenant. Proceed with caution."

It didn't take too long to cross the valley to the Agency Road. By then most of the men at our back had forded the creek. We waited on them to close up. I was sitting Temper, staring up at the rim above the road. Not much cover to speak of, but a man up there wouldn't be seen from below until he come right up to the edge.

And then someone did.

"Major," Sensibaugh said.

Thornburgh looked up and saw the Indian. Then he said, "Good. This is going to work."

I kept my eyes on the rider atop the rim. He clutched his rifle in his right hand, the reins in his left. The sun hit off the copper bands on his arms. I remembered the first time I'd seen him up on that buckskin. Him and his horse still struck you like they were one creature—like something out of a fable.

Noah said, "He's got his war paint on, Tory."

"Looks good on him."

The major called out to us. "You know that Indian?"

Noah said the name. "Chief Jack."

Up yonder, Sowerwick rode up alongside him. I said to myself, war paint just makes that one look more ugly.

Lieutenant Sensibaugh called back an order. Down the line the men dismounted and spread out in the grass. Some moved up on our flanks to cover the major.

Noah said, "What do you make of Sowerwick's hat?"

Something made that hat important. Wouldn't come to me. I heard rifles being cocked. The blood started to sound in my ears. Out of the corner of my eye I saw the major step his horse forward, shout up to the rim.

"Major Thomas T. Thornburgh, Third Cavalry, United States Army, out of Ft. Steele, Wyoming. We come peacefully and wish to meet with you."

Suddenly it come to me.

"That's Charlie Wheelwright's hat," I said.

Then I heard the shot. It might have been one of our own men off on the flank, or it could have been some Indian hidden in the rocks. But as soon as I heard it, I saw Jack swing the Winchester up to his shoulder. I saw the white smoke blow from the muzzle, and then come the crack of the bullet and the cry out of Thornburgh's throat. It was something like the first sound in the word "God." It was drowned out in an instant by the scream of his horse as the major fell and then by the gunfire all around us. Weapons appeared all along the rim—and more from behind the rocks and clumps of brush up and down the Agency Road—and then as Temper wheeled about, I saw more puffs of white smoke blossom on the sand dunes. There wasn't no retreat.

Then I saw men die. Others dropped to one knee and

trained their Spencers on the road without fear—or despite fear. Some dragged the injured and the dead behind the sagebrush or into the tall grass. And there were others who leapt for cover like rabbits and hugged the earth.

Everywhere horses were running and rearing. The ones that went down made cover for soldiers. I saw half a dozen men huddled behind a horse whose legs still churned. Another mount, shot through the chest, got to its feet, keeled over sideways, got up again. Most of the stock that hadn't been hit banded up, fell in behind a big black stud—was it the major's horse?—and pounded off to the north, trailing dust.

Noah—where was Noah? I saw him then—hunkered down in a gully about halfway up the slope to the road, banging away with that Colt of his. Then I reined about and searched the rim with my eyes. Jack was there. Straight up on his pony's back, gazing down on the battle so cool and regal—like he was certain no hunk of lead could harm him. Then our eyes met, and when they did I felt safe, too. No bullet would find either of us. Me and Jack, we were being saved for each other.

Then he surprised me. He smiled. Not what you'd call a grin, exactly, but a smile of pleasure, like he was smiling at something that he knew and I didn't. He clapped his heels to the buckskin, and him and then Sowerwick angled down off the rim—a ten-foot drop almost straight up and down through the slide rock. They landed light as cats.

I whispered, "Just come and get it."

But Jack fooled me again. He whoaed up, sudden-like, and with a wave of his Winchester he sent Sowerwick.

I thought, you canny son of a bitch. In the middle of all this, you find a way to insult me.

But I hadn't long to think on it, for here come the ugly one—howling through the din and the smoke and the flying lead like he'd been born just to kill me. I didn't think much about him either way. It was strange, watching Sowerwick come charging down the slope, and me with no fear in my heart, nor fire in my veins, nor any other sort of passion to speak of—just the cold knowledge that I'd have to brush him aside to get at his boss.

But then I understood why Jack had sent his henchman to do his work. He had no time to spare for the likes of me. For an instant I looked away from Sowerwick and caught a glimpse of Jack on the Agency Road. He was at full gallop, heading south.

To kill me might bring him some satisfaction, but Jack had other business—at White River.

Sowerwick meant to unhorse me and cut my throat. He rode straight through the lead I flung his way. But Sowerwick rode like a wild man and gave a feller no easy shot. After I had emptied my Colt there was nothing left to do but brace myself.

He charged up on my right side, shrieking his war cry and lifting his arm to catch me round the neck. As he struck I bent low, and with both my hands I drove the butt of my gun into his belly. The blow made him grunt and drove him out of the saddle but he drug me along on his way down and I thudded hard onto my shoulder. Before I could gather myself he was on me, and he could wrassle like nothing I'd ever known—arms and hands everywhere and legs that wrapped around me and kept me down there in the dust and give me no way to use my strength. He got me round the chest with his arms locked at my back and my elbows pinned up useless over my head. I could feel his breath in my face and the burning grew in my lungs for lack of air. I had no weapon but my hard head and I butted him once and then again and this time I drew blood and his balance failed him and I pulled him over sidewise and slammed him into the ground.

That cost him his grip, but his hand went for his knife and

he come up waving it. I had mine out and just flung it, and when the blade sunk into Sowerwick's belly, it decided things.

What I needed now was to get back in the saddle. Jack was putting miles between us. The troops were forting up some distance back of where I stood, shooting the stock to make breastworks and drawing up the wagons that had managed to cross Milk Creek. The Utes were still in command of things, but the first shock of the ambush had passed. I caught sight of my Colt and holstered it and found my hat as well, and then behind me Sowerwick got up on his knees and thrust his knife into my side.

I howled a curse at him and tried to strike him with my hand—but he was probably dead by then, for Noah's bullet tore into his back and flung him against me. I stepped back and he fell to the ground. He hadn't let go of the knife. I thought only one thing—that this would keep me from catching Jack.

I pressed my hand to the wound and I was afraid now to lift it. But the blood had hardly soaked through my clothes. Maybe it wasn't too bad. I'd been told the deep wounds burn like fire. This one felt different—no worse than if I'd been hit hard with a hammer or suchlike. And I was still standing, wasn't I? I said to hell with it.

I hoisted up onto Temper's back. It wasn't bad. I kept my head low and galloped along the side of the rise. I shouted, "Nice shot, Uncle. Could have been quicker, though."

"My horse run off," he yelled back. "You're gonna have to catch that Ute yourself."

I stopped and looked back at him. I could tell from what he'd said that he'd seen Jack light out of there, and he knew what it meant if someone didn't stop the Indian before he reached White River.

I shouted, "Try to keep your hair."

I saw him grin, all those funny teeth. Then I took off.

For a mile the noise of the battle followed after. I could hear the warcries and the shouting and the guns, then only the guns, then Temper's hoofbeats and the wind in my ears. I tried to reckon Jack's head start. Ten minutes—maybe a hair less'n that. I had my work cut out.

We covered the five miles to Beaver Springs, where the major had decided he'd water the stock. I slowed a little for Temper to have a blow. Yellowjacket Pass lay just beyond— steep walls and deep shadow. I touched the spurs to my horse and he leapt to it. We dug hard, and I could hear the sound of our gallop—my shouts and Temper's hooves— coming back at us off the high rocks.

We got through the pass unmolested and the canyon widened. I saw Jack's tracks shorten up.

Watch out, now, chief. Old No-Name's comin'.

We had ten miles behind us now. Temper's lungs were heaving, but he was not a horse to give in to things.

We rounded an outcrop of rock and the ground fell away so's I could see down the canyon.

I saw dust. Thinning but hanging there, no more than a quarter-mile before us. The road dipped and the canyon took another turn. There was no seeing past it. But I knew who it was that raised the cloud, and I slapped my horse on the rump and we were hell-bent.

Two hundred fifty yards and into the dust now, flying, and if you listened close under the pounding of Temper's hooves you could hear another sound—other hooves. And then the canyon walls fell away and we broke into the sun, the light dazzling on the plateau yonder and the sky deep blue and huge and empty, and down there on the Agency Road, raising a fresh plume of dust in his wake, was Jack.

I let out a holler born of all the fear and hate and hopelessness I'd stored up that day. I guess Jack heard it— that or my horse's hoofbeats—for I saw him turn to look over his shoulder. It was too far to see his face, but I could guess his thoughts. He must be thinking how Sowerwick couldn't get the job done, how he has to do everything himself. He reined his horse off the road and into open country. I bent low on Temper's neck and pressed him down the slope and I said, "Okay, boy, get him, get him," and that old range pony of mine gave me all he had.

In a mile we cut his lead in half. Soon we raced up on the place where his lodges used to be. That left but three miles or so till White River Agency—but long before we got there I knew we would likely come onto Douglas's lookouts. If that happened, and they took word back with them, it wouldn't matter if I caught Jack or not.

When you're on horseback chasing a man, like as not you won't hit him with a rifle shot. 'Specially if him and his horse are dodging amongst the bushes and leaping over rocks and gullies. But I held the advantage coming up on his tail, and I was in range, so I yanked my Winchester from its scabbard and levered a shell into the chamber. What I wanted bad was to fight this Indian—to beat him hand-to-hand. But I might not catch him soon enough for that. And anyhow, there was more at stake this time than pride—more to win than Josie's bonnet. This time it was her life.

One lucky shot, I thought, and you and me, we're done. One dose of luck is all I need.

Then Temper took a bad step, and fell.

I flew over his head and it seemed I was in the air forever. I landed hard. A long time I lay there stunned, and then the pain called out to me from the wound in my side. I reached down to my ribs and pulled my fingers up to have a look. I thought, this time you're tore up good. I eased up so I could look to the southward, but the dust was too thick. All I could hear were Jack's hoofbeats trailing off.

I thought, You ain't givin' in.

I gathered myself together and got to my feet. *If you can stand, you can walk. Better yet, ride. Find your horse.*

I found him by a patch of fireweed, standing on three legs, blowing fast and shallow. I knelt by his side and felt his ankle.

Then I stood up and patted his nose and scratched his ears. I touched his neck and his withers where the dust and the sweat stood out. "Now you done it," I said, soft-like.

I knew it pained him every minute I waited. I wasn't thinking too clear but my pistol was in my hand, and I slipped a cartridge into the cylinder and held the muzzle up to Temper's head. I petted him again. Afterward the sound kind of hung there, and then I couldn't hardly stand it, it was so quiet.

I took the canteen and my cash and all the ammunition from my saddle. I come across the old buffalo tail I carried everywhere, and I tucked it into my belt. Then I went back and retrieved my hat and my Winchester. I had a ways to go yet.

I followed the river, west by northwest, don't know how long. My side throbbed bad and it got so I just drug one foot after the other. My mind wasn't working proper. Sleepy. Seemed to me I'd been going at it a while. Hadn't slept much since Sunday night—here it was, what, Tuesday. Been riding and fighting and chasing Indians all day, had fearful things to think about. The hole in my ribs still wet. And Temper . . . . Noah would call it bad cards. Noah. I ought to just lay down here. Down by the box elder, watch the branches tremble, wait for the leaves to fall. Always liked fall. Best to curl up right here. River tricklin' by, wood smoke in the air . . .

There shouldn't have been no wood smoke—not where I lay. I don't know if I smelled it and then slept, or whether it was the first thing come to me when I woke. But I was on my feet now, sudden-like, everything sharp—the glow of the sun all but lost behind the hills, the cool of the evening here, the breeze in my face, blowing out of the northwest, pungent. I ran toward the smoke.

I hadn't far to go. Just around the bend in fact. How long had it been since me and Bill Nunan had turned this bend with my uncle in tow? And now here I was again—back where all this started, back where Shadrach Price had took off his hat and grinned at us and said him and his friends was irrigatin'. Same spot it was, only this time I had to slink into the ditch so's not to be seen by Indians. And this time I had something different to fret over.

The flames roared over Nathan Meeker's creation. I stood there staring, feeling the heat on the wind even at this distance, and wondering if there was a white person left alive.

There wasn't no telling from here. I could see figures moving around, dark and blurry against the flames. They were carrying torches to spread the fire. I listened for voices, but from where I was all I could hear was the crackle of sap boiling in the burning wood, and the hiss of the fire on the tar roofs and the roar of the flames licking out of the windows. Yonder past the warehouse I could see the second floor of the boardinghouse. I saw the flames in my room— the room where we'd nursed Uncle Noah back to life, and where he'd stood in the window and sprayed the street with gunfire to save my skin. The room where Josie and I had shared secrets whilst my uncle slept—and where I'd kissed her.

I'd met Jack in that room.

I crept along the ditch to where I could look down the length of Josie's Lane, but there weren't much to see for the smoke and the darkness. So I climbed out of there and crept through the dirt toward the boardinghouse. I sought cover back of the woodpile. Something was sort of draped over the cordwood. It was the body of Shad Price. He'd took a blow to the left side of the face and the blood was in his hair. Maybe they'd put bullets in him—I couldn't see.

The heat was too much to be standing there long. I drew back and had a look in through the kitchen door. Two boys were dead at the table, facedown.

I moved around back, along Meeker Street, and slunk

through the shadows along the wall of the boardinghouse. Across the way the icehouse was on fire. Down the street where the livestock pens had been, they'd pulled the planks off the fence posts and piled them up and put the torch to them. Nearby on the ground was another body. I run over to it.

I couldn't tell who it was. His feet were tied together. I took aholt of his shoulder and turned him over. He'd been drug over hard ground till the flesh had been torn from his face. I wiped the mud away with my fingers and saw his bared teeth, like a grin.

I looked around me. It was grown full dark, the light of the flames casting shadows and bright spots that moved with the smoke. I thought, This is like being in hell. I listened close—a lot of Indians shouting back and forth, the sound of wagons and animals moving. I heard the crack of timbers giving way and then the roof of the boardinghouse fell in, embers blowing into the air. Waste and hopelessness took hold of my heart.

Whose fault was this? Jack? Or Douglas? Major Thornburgh for not taking heed? Or Nathan Meeker? Or any of us? I couldn't say. Even in the darkness, half-scorched by the heat and choking in the smoke, I didn't know who to blame. It was like we'd all of us been swept up in something vast and terrible. What we'd intended didn't much matter. The land we'd been born on, the color we'd been born with, what we'd been taught a man ought to be, or who it was we'd come to love—these things made us what we were. We just did what we had to do.

But like Uncle Noah had said, you go with what you got. What I had just then was my Winchester and my Colt pistol, and a pocketful of .45 caliber cartridges that fit either one.

I had me something to shoot at, too.

The whole bunch—Jack and Douglas leading on horseback, Colorow just behind them—was coming round the corner. Eight other mounted warriors flanking two wagons and a buckboard. Supplies in the wagons, tarpaulins over them. Two more braves in the rear, handling the spare horses—each of them edgy, not liking the fire. The light caught in the horses' eyes. I saw into the buckboard. A Ute by the name of Pauvitz drove. Behind him, Shadrach's wife Flora Ellen with her children huddled to her, and Arvilla, and Josie. Another brave, Ahutupuwit, in the wagon with them. They didn't seem hurt—more like they were stunned. Nathan Meeker wasn't there. I wondered if the women had been made to watch.

I tried to think like Jack would've thought. The Ute lodges, with their women and young'uns and old folks, were safely removed. The army had been foiled. Meeker and his Greeley boys were all dead. Jack had made his point. What he'd want now would be to head for Grand River. That meant southward. But his fighting men were still tussling with the cavalry north of here—so he lacked his strength. All Jack had was a dozen braves or less—and they were really Douglas's men, not his. So he'd have to play it safe—move quick, hold onto his captives, keep to the wild country.

I crouched back of the water trough and thought it over. If I were Jack, I couldn't expect the long knives to stay tied up forever. Might be they were already on their way. Time to get rolling, right now—couldn't afford to tarry this side of White River—and I sure as hell wouldn't want any surprises to hold me up.

So I knew what I had to do.

They were moving up the street in my direction. I checked to see my Colt was loaded, careful not to click the cylinder too loud. I holstered it. Then I took my Winchester in hand, breathed in and out just once, and swung out from behind the trough in full view of Jack and the others.

They weren't ten paces in front of me. I come up out of the smoke with my Winchester blazing at my hip. I hoped Jack got a good look at who it was. But he had plenty to keep him busy. His pony reared up and flung him backwards. I snapped off one clean shot at him and fired two more as he went over and I hoped to hell I'd gotten the job done, but there was no way of knowing as I had my hands full with the others.

I let one go at Douglas and missed, but my next shot blew Colorow down and I could see they were all too surprised to move so I charged right into them, howling like I was some crazy Ute myself. I didn't think about odds—didn't think about nothing but firing off a shot point-blank into the chest of the nearest brave and then the next, and of running and dodging while I let fly at another and then another. They might have seen me plain and they might not, what with the smoke all around and the flames at my back. But they were each of them lit up bright and clear, the sweat streaking their faces, the eyes wide with wonderment, so close that even on the dead run I couldn't hardly miss.

I got away and found cover back of the schoolhouse. By now they were off their horses and firing my way. They were spreading out, too, losing themselves in the darkness.

I hunkered down by the wall, reloading and catching my breath. I thought, the easy part's over. But you don't want to start thinking. Just keep moving, tie 'em up. Don't even have to kill any. Just stay alive. All they really want to be is away and gone.

I wondered if I had killed Jack. But it nagged at me—maybe I hadn't. Damn horse of his. I knew I'd got Colorow, and I'd put lead into others as well. I thought—For you, Frank Dresser, for all you boys. Then I thought of the women and how things might go worse for them. But I only thought of that for a fraction, for bullets crashed all around me and then one seared my head just above the ear.

I ducked round the south corner of the schoolhouse and more lead come flying. And then from across Josie's Lane, knife held overhead and his war cry fierce and frightful, Antelope come running for me. I fanned my pistol at him and missed twice before he reached me, but I ducked my head and threw him over my back and he hit the schoolhouse wall so that when I spun around and kicked at him there was no way he could dodge the blow and he took it full in the belly. I got off a shot just as he grabbed at my gun hand and I think the bullet caught him in the hip, for he spun around and down and could only grope for me with his knife, hissing like a snake.

Others were coming for me now. I run slant-wise across the street toward the Meekers' house. I reckoned it for the first building the Utes had set afire, for nothing remained beyond the shell of the thing and the chimney—the flames still licking at the back and the side walls but the front wall and the porch already gone. I heard guns to my rear and my left. The wind was shifting round and I couldn't count on smoke for cover out here. I run around back and saw that one of the doors to the cellar had been torn loose. There was just that burning back wall before me and open ground on all sides. In a few seconds the Utes would have me out here in the open.

It was one of them choices where you'll probably die either way. I dove into the cellar and pulled the door after. Soon enough they'd figure out that I was down here—but then they'd have to come and get me. And if that door was pulled open and an Indian showed his face, I'd blow it off.

It was black in there but for a little moonlight through the cracks. The Utes had already cleaned the place out. I laid back on the dirt floor, looking up at the doors. My side ached plenty. I had bruises I hadn't even kept track of, and a chunk of my scalp was gone. I thought, You'll probably lose the rest of it soon enough.

What I heard then was the entire rear wall of Meeker's house collapse in a heap of flaming timber—right on top of where I was. The dirt and the dust and burning embers come roaring in through the gaps between the slats. There was no light at all and no air to breath and my first thought was to push the doors loose, Indians or not, and get the hell out of there. But I couldn't. Where I'd seen moonlight a minute previous, I saw only the red glow of flames, and the weight atop the doors made it hopeless to move them.

I hadn't much strength left, anyway. There was no room even to stand. I was on my knees, trying to think. I'd done all I could. Nothing left to draw on.

I don't know how much time passed. Judging by the sound, the fire overhead was burning out. I could hear the crackle of embers. Then I heard a voice out there, where it seemed so far away now, where people saw stars, and breathed air, and stood up straight.

It was Chief Jack.

Some other Indian was with him. I knew that voice, too. Douglas.

So they both were alive. I knew my shot had missed the older one—but Jack?

I heard someone poking through the rubble. Douglas said something in Ute, likely telling Jack there was no more time to waste on me. Jack answered in English.

He said, "Let us add more timber to what is here. We will bury the Nameless One alive and give him time to ponder his death."

And then I got to listen to the sound of other voices calling back and forth, and the wagons and the animals forming up again, moving away now, and then silence.

CHAPTER 13

I SPENT the night closed up in the earth like someone already dead. But I wasn't gonna give in to it—not to the cold that stiffened my bruised shoulders nor to the lonesomeness in my heart, nor even to the fear that come creeping into the cellar with me. I kind of welcomed the fear, just as I welcomed the burning in my side and the gnaw in my stomach and the way my tongue had swole up and tasted like blood. Anything that pained me served to keep me awake—and I needed to keep awake in case the army arrived, so's I could let them know I was down here in this hole. Then they could dig me out. Then I could get after Jack.

Late in the night I heard the howling of the prairie wolves. Time passed and they moved closer, till finally I heard them scratch at the boards overhead, and move off, and then I heard them yapping round the bodies out yonder till they'd set the pecking order. Then I tried not to listen no more.

I must have dozed some. When I awakened the light come stabbing down through the slats so's it hurt my eyes. There weren't room to stretch. Even if there had been, I wasn't sure I could get up. My shirt was soaked with sweat and my teeth were chattering.

Then I heard the wagon.

I was gonna call out to it, but I caught myself. I heard the rig come to a stop, but I couldn't say who it was. If it was the army, there'd be more than just this one. And if it was a scout—well, scouts don't drive wagons. I wondered if it wasn't Jack himself, come round again just to see if old No-Name had had it.

I could play possum till he pulled open the cellar doors,

and then kill him with my gun. I fancied the thought. But if it wasn't him? Nobody else would have much call to check the cellar. I might just find myself left behind.

So I shouted, "Hey!"

Didn't work. There wasn't much strength in me but I pounded my rifle butt against the doors to raise as much of a racket as I could. Sounded plenty loud from where I was— loud enough so's to make my head throb worse than it already did. But whoever it was out there, he was in no hurry to get to me.

I figured maybe he's playing games. I shouted again, and then stopped to listen. Strange how it was. I couldn't hear him, but I could feel him.

He knew how to move quiet. So quiet maybe you had to be in the earth to know he was moving over it. I felt pretty certain there was an Indian up there.

A board moved. I heard it being drug off the pile, scraping against the others. One by one they all come away. The sun was bright through the gaps they left and I knew, whoever it was, he was right there. I crouched hard by the wall, pressing myself into the cold damp earth, waiting on him to throw open the doors. My Colt was in hand. If I was gonna die today, I was gonna take this last one with me.

I said, "Come on in, you son of a bitch."

But he didn't. I waited on his shadow to move across the slats, but he weren't having none of it. The first move would have to be mine. I thought about it, and then I gathered up what strength remained and flung myself up through the doors and into the sunshine.

After being in the dark for all of a night and half of a day, I was blinded by the noonday sun. All I could see was a bright blaze of light like fire. I heard the click of a hammer drawn back. I spun at the sound, and as I did I could just make out who it was.

It wasn't no Indian. This was a white man in a red woolen shirt and buckskin jacket. He had snow-white hair to his shoulders and a ragged beard. He held his gun steady. The left hand moved into a pocket of his jumper and fetched forth a piece of paper, all folded and tattered.

I lowered my weapon and took it. By the time I got it flattened out it just about fell asunder. What it said was that this feller could hear but he couldn't speak none. It said he'd be pleased to write out what it was he had to say. And it said his name was Wolf Miller.

It was dusk when the army showed up. We were done with the burying, the Dutchman and me, and when we heard them coming we were roasting antelope steaks on a fire by the river bank. We'd set there a spell—him cradling his pipe in those gnarled old hands, and me watching the clouds move in over the Danforth Hills. We'd seen death up close this day, and what we'd seen leaves its mark on a man. We two had buried men we'd known and come to like, men dead and defiled at the hands of Indians, and picked over by wolves and magpies. The sight of cavalry was the first thing we'd had to cheer us since late that morning, when I'd told the Dutchman who I was and he'd lowered his gun and grinned at me through his whiskers.

He'd wrote me a note that asked if Douglas had done this. I told him yes, and he let me know it saddened him. Douglas and him were friends. He'd known Antelope and Loud Cry when they were naked little boys playing with toy hatchets. He'd known Meeker, too, though not as well, and he'd warned him of the crop he was sowing. But it didn't make no difference.

When the company drew up it was Lieutenant Sensibaugh in command. Next to him, looking worn but still breathing, Uncle Noah. Our eyes met. We let that say it all.

The rest were a ragged bunch. Three of them rode mules. Their faces were blank and they looked dead in the eyes, but the smell of our steaks seemed to rouse them. Turned out that during the battle the Utes had fired the supply train.

These men had been without grub for more than a day, during which time they'd fought free of the Utes, buried their dead, got themselves reorganized and rode twenty-five miles to the agency. So the first thing we did was, we fed them. The Dutchman's wagon was loaded down with twelve hundred pounds of field-dressed venison and antelope. That was what Nathan Meeker had contracted for, but he wouldn't miss it now.

They spread out on the grass to sleep. I said to Sensibaugh, "Where are the rest of 'em?"

"They'll be along," he said. "They're afoot."

I thought, That couldn't be right. "You had three hundred animals."

"I have twelve now."

He told us what had happened up by Milk Creek. After Colonel Thornburgh had been killed, his second-in-command took a bullet in the eye. That left Sensibaugh in charge. The troops forted up in the middle of the valley, killing their animals to make breastworks. The Utes were satisfied just to snipe away at them from the hills to the north and south. Mostly nothing much would happen—then a flurry of shots would sound, and a man would cry out. It went on that way till dark.

At night two men had volunteered to ride through the line and try for Rawlins.

I said, "Did they make it?"

"Hard to say. But we didn't hear shots. That's a good sign."

Noah scratched his eyebrow, thoughtful-like. "Even if they got through," he said, "it'll be a week before reinforcements make it back. Ain't that right?"

That stirred the Lieutenant. "Very true. That's why—once the remainder of my command catches up with us—we'll fetch them a hot meal and some rest. Then we'll pursue the Utes southward."

I said, "On foot?"

"Mostly. We've got arms and plenty of ammunition." He

waved a hand over toward the Dutchman's wagon. "Plenty of food. They left us a perfect trail up by the ford. Lord knows we've learned their intentions, so this time the fight'll be even."

The Dutchman blew hard. You could tell he thought this was foolishness. I wasn't so sure. I was ready to fight Utes.

Still I asked, "Don't you have to wait on orders or reinforcements or suchlike?"

Sensibaugh looked me straight in the eye and I could see this wasn't open to argument. "Bowhunter, I've got thirty-nine men to avenge. That's thirty-nine men killed by these savages—plus nine bodies you buried here today, two little children they've kidnapped, and three women who for God's sake may have been raped and butchered by now. We'll not wait. Not while the trail is warm."

"Way I heard it," Noah said, "Wolf Miller here has knowed Ouray and Douglas and the rest of that bunch for years. Thought to ask him what to do?"

The lieutenant's voice rose so quick that one or two of the troopers nearby sat up. "I'll remind you, mister, I don't have to ask anyone . . ."

"Just thinkin'," Noah said, slow and quiet-like, "Seems to me you're fixin' to head deeper into reservation lands, where the Utes know the country and you don't. You'll have cavalry walkin' around on foot. You ain't got no orders, and you don't know much about Indians. Like as not you're gonna blunder in there and get everybody killed."

"I have orders . . ."

"Had orders. You were supposed to protect all the folks that Tory and the Dutchman here just buried. You failed at that. Now don't make it worse."

"You're interfering in the mission of this command. Move off before I have you arrested."

Noah got up. He'd spoke his mind and wasn't about to press matters. I walked off a ways with him.

We sat with the Dutchman by the fire and Noah said, "I'm right sorry about Temper, son."

I was, too. There was plenty of things for me and Noah to grieve over—his arm, Colonel Thornburgh and his men, Nathan Meeker and his boys. But we didn't speak of the old man or any of the others. Not even of Josie. I told Noah of my chase after Jack and the scrape I'd had here at White River, and how me and the Dutchman reckoned Douglas and Jack were heading south for Grand River country, maybe to hide out through the winter. Noah told me that back at Milk Creek the Utes had had the bluecoats pinned down, but couldn't finish them off. Like as not they'd decided to retreat further into the reservation before more soldiers came. Then they could fight it out on their ground.

"From what I've seen of the Utes," I said, "they're the ones who know how to make war."

The Dutchman nodded at that. It was full dark now and I could see his face in the fire, brooding and silent. We were off some distance from the lieutenant. There were troopers camped all about, and pickets out beyond. There wasn't a one of 'em looked awake. The Dutchman fetched forth a sheet of paper and commenced to write. Took him a while, too, puffing thoughtful-like on his short-stemmed pipe. When he finished with his note he handed it to me and moved off, like this here was something for me and Noah to chew over without him.

The note laid things out as the Dutchman saw them. He said that Douglas was in hot water, and Jack, too. Both were chiefs among the White River Utes, but the chief of all the Utes was Ouray. Ouray had spent his life keeping Utes and white men from killing each other. He knew there were plenty of white men who craved an excuse to put the tribe out of Colorado. The massacre at White River would be just the ticket. Once Ouray thought that through, he might propose to cut his losses.

I stopped reading. "How might he do that?"

Noah run his hand over the stubble on his face. Then he smiled. "This Dutchman is a clever feller."

"How so?"

"Keep readin'."

Wolf Miller had knowed Ouray a long time. He figured the chief would reckon it like so—that human beings came and went. You could lose one or two and carry on. But the land was sacred. If the Utes lost all their lands, they were through. Give Ouray a little room to work, the Dutchman wrote, and he'd free up the women and turn the killers over to the authorities. That might cool off the hotheads in Denver and maybe pull the Utes' coals from the fire.

I looked up again. "You mean that one Ute chief is gonna turn in two other Ute chiefs? How are we gonna arrange that?"

Noah said, "We ain't. But I'll bet the Dutchman is."

"And free up the women, too?"

"Ouray ain't got a choice. If he don't free up the women, nothing else he does is gonna make a difference."

I wasn't sure of all this, and said so.

Noah said, "Think on it, son. The Dutchman will tell Ouray it's his only chance. That's our best shot at gettin' the women back alive. Maybe our only shot."

He meant all the women and the young'uns, too, but he knew well what was most on my mind. What I wanted to do was charge in there and take Josie, the way Lieutenant Sensibaugh intended. And I had other business as well. But I thought hard on it like Noah said, and I said, "All right, Uncle. What do we do now?"

He looked over where the Dutchman's wagon stood. The riding horse was gone.

"It's already been done."

Later on some feeling brung me awake. Noah's bedroll was open but he wasn't in it. I fetched my holster and picked my way through the troops, then cut over to the right and circled past what was left of the agency warehouse. I come out onto Josie's Lane.

I said, "Hello, Noah."

"I was just thinkin', son." It was like he'd been expecting me. "Seemed to me a mite less complicated when we was herding cows."

He sounded tired. I said, "How's the arm?"

"Ain't too bad. How many Indians did you kill here last night?"

"Dunno. Three. Four, maybe."

"Will that do ya?"

I didn't know how to take that. But I knew the answer. "No, sir. There's still Jack."

He took the last draw off his smoke and flicked the butt away. "It's no good, Tory. It's like a poison inside you. It'll kill your heart."

"Noah, I ain't got nothin' going for me but hatred."

"Looks that way now, don't it? But it ain't so."

"What else have I got?"

"That girl's still alive."

"Maybe."

"She's alive. And you want her back. It ain't hatred that ought to be drivin' you, son."

I looked away from him. "I don't reckon I know what it is."

He said, "Things ain't never simple—not when it comes to men and women. Them books Bill Nunan reads, 'tain't like that. Never been like that."

We walked further down Josie's Lane. A gap broke in the clouds and the moon shone through. We come up on the boardinghouse. Just a pile of black shadows is all that was left. The smell of burnt wood was sharp in your nostrils. The bodies I'd found in the kitchen—they'd been Thompson and Hickett—two boys taking supper. My thoughts were crowding in on me. I wanted to run or drink whiskey or shoot at something.

Noah said, "You ain't mentioned your pa."

If he'd thought that I'd forgot, I hadn't. "I dunno, Uncle. All I been doin' is what looked right to me."

"Don't reckon you could have done otherwise."

"Maybe Bill was right."

He brushed that aside. "You spoke to the Dutchman?"

I had, that afternoon. He'd last seen Pa in the spring, near Tourmaline. Pa had been camped no more'n ten miles from there. We must've trailed right by him.

"Wolf said he'd guide us back there, after all this is over."

"Did you tell him Tourmaline was burnt to the ground?" Noah asked.

"Yes. He said it baffled him. Said the Utes weren't the sort to kill white folks and burn towns."

We caught each other's eye, and then we laughed. It was the first time we'd laughed, me and Uncle Noah, since I didn't know when.

Part 3
To North Park

CHAPTER 14

WE fetched up into high plateau country, and though it was October now the sun felt hotter than that. It looked to us like the main body of Utes, the ones that had fought at Milk Creek, were keeping to the Grand River trail southward toward the old squaw camp on Piceance Creek. We had no way of knowing if Jack and Douglas were headed for there, but we hadn't much else to go on. We trailed thataways for more than a week. Whenever we found sign, it was fresh. Some of the Utes had to be lagging back to watch us, but we never saw them, and while they had more than one chance to lay in wait for us, they never tried it.

After a spell of this Noah had them figured. "They're just keepin' a safe distance," he said. "Probably ain't sure what to do with us."

I cut him a plug. "Waitin' on orders, do you reckon?"

"More'n likely. Says to me they ain't met up with their chiefs as yet, though they expect to. Good sign."

We got to the old squaw camp. Nothing much to be found, save for the mark of Indians having come and gone—Indians who didn't mind if we followed. We moved upstream and beyond the headwaters of Piceance Creek and then down off Roan Plateau into the valley of Grand River. After all that high desert, this here was plush country—plenty of good grass after so much juniper and piñon and scrub brush.

We moved westward downstream on the Grand, and next afternoon we forded that river where it shallowed out under some red-gray sandstone bluffs. To our left was the north rim of Grand Mesa. Not a one of us had seen Grand Mesa previous to this, but there weren't much else it could be. It just went up and up.

Lieutenant Sensibaugh turned in the saddle. "The men will rest here," he said. "Then we'll find a trail up to the top."

"No, we won't," Noah said.

"And why not?"

" 'Cause of all them Indians on the shelf there."

The lieutenant's head swiveled around to take them all in. And then back around again to see the band that was out in the open behind us—maybe fifty braves ahorseback. They'd been trailing us downstream.

Noah said, "Before you get us killed, Lieutenant, hang fire a minute."

Sensibaugh looked back at him, and I thought I saw something in his glance said he wouldn't mind giving up this business of commanding soldiers. Noah, though, was as steady in his eyes as ever I'd seen a man. He said it again—"Just hang fire"—and I thought he might kill the lieutenant right there if he didn't do as he was told.

Two Ute riders galloped down from the rocks. They come forth into full view and reined in. Didn't recognize either one, so I reckoned them for Uncompahgre Utes—Ouray's band. They were wary, but no one leveled a weapon at them so they stepped their ponies our way.

One was a wrinkly little feller who called himself Shavano. Said he was Ouray's war chief. He had a grave air to him, like the Utes had taken to turning out Presbyterian ministers. The other was Sapovanero. He had him a soft, meaty sort of face, tiny black eyes. Long braids.

The two of them just set their horses, comfortable-like, and what they did was discuss the weather. I'd heard it all before, too—from Wolf Miller back at the agency. He said the long summer had the game confused. Said he'd been held up in the hunt this year because the antelope didn't know when to come down off their summer ranges.

Which was fascinating except I had other things on my

mind. Someone was gonna have to come out and ask these Indians what they were up to. And since no one else seemed likely to do it, I just said, "Look, you two seen a bunch of your White River friends come through here with some white women?"

Shavano looked at me. The brown face stayed grave, but I thought I saw something like a smile in his eyes.

He said, "You are the Nameless One."

That brung me up short. "Some call me that."

Noah was grinning now. He said, "Word carries."

"You come with us," Shavano said. "You and your uncle. The others stay."

'Course, I wasn't about to say no, considering the fifty Ute warriors at our back and all the rest up on the rocks.

Lieutenant Sensibaugh said, "We'll make our camp right here and wait on your return."

As if there was a choice, I thought.

There was a stream atop Grand Mesa called Plateau Creek. We must have been at upwards of eight or nine thousand feet when we reached it, gazing over the valley it cut through the high desert. The shadows were long about this hour, but the creek sparkled like copper in the sun. There was grass and willows and berry bushes by the water—and about two dozen tepees belonging to Douglas and Jack.

"What do you think, Noah?"

"Dunno. Don't see the women."

Nor did I. There were ponies and sheep set out to graze, and young'uns and dogs chasing about amongst the lodges, and squaws at work with supper, the smell of meat cooking on the fire. But I didn't see what I come for. I didn't see Josie or the others, not any sign of them.

"Look there," Noah said. He pointed out a wagon I hadn't seen previous. Pair of wagons, in fact, and as we drew nigh there were horses, too. Three good-sized saddle mounts hitched to a wagon yoke—not the sort of Ute ponies we'd come to know. Closer in I peered round the biggest of the lodges—and past the half-dozen braves that set there to guard the door flap—and I could make out two other horses as well.

"I think those are the Dutchman's there."

Noah said, "Seems like it."

"And the wagons? Ouray?"

"Maybe."

"You don't think we'll need a ticket to get into this, do you?"

"Don't reckon so."

Ouray here already? Made sense. Far as we could calculate, we'd come some hundred and twenty miles south from White River. That left us maybe eighty miles north of Ouray's home on the Uncompahgre. Chances were that Ouray wouldn't have had to wait on Wolf Miller to tell him something had happened at Milk Creek and White River. There'd have been Ute runners to tell him that. So he'd have had time to get the word by now and ride on up here. That is, if he was amind to.

And the other horses? We were still pondering over that when we reached the big tepee. We drew a crowd of young'uns and squaws, none of them edgy or hateful—just curious as usual. Sapovanero swung down and went inside the tepee, and then the flap lifted and out come a Ute in full regalia—buckskins and fancy beadwork, a headdress with bear claws dangling and eagle feathers trailing behind. A bright sash of yellow cotton round his waist, a knife in a sheath stitched with more beads.

You didn't have to be told this was Ouray.

He was sick, though. He wasn't no older than forty-five, by my reckoning, but the whites of his eyes were stained yellow-brown and there was a sallow look to him. I'd been told this Ouray was built like a bull, but now he was skinnied-down to half what you'd expect.

Yet the power was there. It come from inside him. This was

the man who'd outthought white men for twenty years, who'd held his people together by force of will alone. He fixed his eye on me and I could feel it like a weight. I felt like I had to straighten my back and breathe deep just to stay the same size in the saddle. I hardly noticed at first who followed him out of the tepee, but Wolf Miller stood there now, all grave and thoughtful but nodding to let me know things was all right. And at the Dutchman's back, another white man, taller and lankier, dressed in black broadcloth. Gray hair and craggy features, and smile lines around the eyes.

This here was the chairman of the Governor's Ute Disposition Committee. Wood Gettys.

We settled in around the fire. Gettys whispered to me and Uncle Noah. "The women are all right. Ouray will deliver five Utes up for trial. Douglas, Nicaagat, Loud Cry, Ahutupuwit, and Pauvitz."

"What about Colorow and Antelope?" I asked.

"You killed them at White River."

I'd no way of knowing, of course. Whatever bodies there'd been following that set-to, the Utes had carted them off.

"How many did I kill?"

"Five."

I kept still but my eyes moved around the tepee. It seemed like every Indian in there was watching me. It was a chilly sort of feeling. Ouray was down in our circle, along with Shavano and another Uncompahgre called Yanko. The inside of the tepee was lined with braves—all of them standing, the fire glinting off their carbines.

Gettys said to me, "Keep your own counsel through this. We'll talk later."

Ouray took up where things had let off. He said, "I want no reprisals."

Gettys said, "You assure me the women have suffered no indignities?"

"This I am told."

"At no time were their persons violated in any way?"

"Douglas tells me this."

Silence for a spell. Then Gettys said, "Douglas and Nicaa-gat and the three others will be tried for the murders of the agent and his staff. This will satisfy the needs of justice."

"There will be no reprisals against my people?"

"Not if the citizens of Colorado feel that justice has been served."

Wolf Miller raised his hands and signed. Ouray grunted, and then turned back to Gettys. "My friend reminds me, justice does not mean the same thing to all men. Some will want to see all the Utes suffer for what a few have done."

"Turn these five over, and you will have done all you can. You will be respected for freeing the captives and turning the murderers over for trial."

"If you call them murderers," Ouray said, "what need for trial?"

Gettys smiled. "You are a wise chief, Ouray. You will cut your losses."

"And the long knives?" Ouray said. "They will want our blood, to avenge their foolishness at Milk Creek."

Gettys glanced over at the Dutchman. "We've thought through that, Wolf and I. You will turn Douglas and the others over to the cavalry that are now pinned down below Grand Mesa. They will escort the five Utes to trial. The army will have its share of glory."

"And this Lieutenant Sensibaugh, who leads like a woman? You would not even have him at this council, for fear he would say the wrong words."

Gettys grinned this time. "Lieutenant Sensibaugh is a hero."

Ouray nodded. He knew white folk, this one. He spoke a few words in Ute to Shavano. "Who will speak for us?"

"This I pledge to you," Gettys said. "A public statement of appreciation to you from the governor. A civilian trial for the defendants. Transportation for you to the trial, and an opportunity for you to make your own statement to the press."

The Dutchman scribbled a note and handed it to Ouray. The chief read it out loud. "The President must promise that the Utes will keep their reservation lands in Colorado."

Gettys looked hard from the chief to the Dutchman. But he nodded firmly. Then he said, "I'll do what I can."

"Where are the women, Wood?"

"Twelve miles up Plateau Creek, at the main camp. They'll be removed in the morning."

"Have you seen them?"

"I have, Tory. They're all right."

"Josie, too?"

"She's all right, son."

"Where's Jack?"

"Ouray's got him and the rest under guard, down at the other end of the camp."

"Whose is he—yours or theirs?"

"He's being held by Ouray on behalf of the government of the United States. That's the deal."

"I want him, Wood."

"What's that mean?"

"Just what I say."

"Can't have him. He's my responsibility."

"If you turn him over to the army tomorrow, and they ship him off to Ft. Steele or somewheres like that, I might never get at him."

"What's it matter to you?"

"You know the answer to that."

"So it's romance. I envy you your passion, son. But he's gonna hang. It's required. You'll have your justice."

"What's that the Dutchman said back there, that justice comes across different to different folks? I've got to dole this out myself."

"I can't help you."

"It's politics stoppin' you, ain't it?"

"Sure it's politics. Politics is what we're bankin' on to get us out of this fix. Politics is what's gonna save that fool Sensibaugh and his men. Politics saved your girl's life."

"It's gonna save Jack's, too."

"What makes you say that?"

"Just a guess. They'll lock him up somewheres, let this blow over. Hangin' him and the others, that would just give the whites a taste of blood, and rile up the Utes even further."

"So what happens instead?"

"Things cool off some. Then one day, come next summer, maybe, when hardly anyone's paying it much mind, they'll bring in more soldiers. This time they'll plan it right, and just like so they'll move the Utes out of Colorado."

"You learn this game too fast, son, you'll grow jaded."

"I'm just trying to think like Jack would. He's known all along what's in the wind."

"And you think he expects not to hang."

"I think that's part of the deal with Ouray. Ouray's too much of a chief to throw his compadres on the fire. Not for politics."

"You've got it down about halfway, Tory. Men do plenty on that account. But in this instance you're right. Jack won't hang."

"Then he'll have to fight me. You can arrange for that, can't you, Wood?"

"What's become of you, son?"

"Can't rightly say, Wood. Maybe I got that streak of mayhem runnin' through me, like you do. But I know that Jack and me—ain't neither of us gonna rest till the other's dead. That's about the size of it."

"Then I guess it's up to Jack."

Gettys left me so's to go talk it over with Ouray. I'd called on him for a favor. More of a favor than he'd wanted to do me—more, probably, than he thought right to do. But he'd done it. If he'd turned me down I'd have gone about it some other way.

Noah and the Dutchman had a pot of coffee on. The Dutchman pointed his pipe for me to pour some for myself. I told them what me and Gettys had spoken of.

He said, "Wolf here has been over to see the women. They're in good shape."

"I'm glad of that."

"You ought to go see her."

"Afterward," I said.

"Might be no need to tangle with Jack if you talk to Josie first."

I didn't speak.

"Maybe you don't want to be talked out of it," he said. "Easier just to fight than to think about things."

"Thinking ain't gonna rid me of him."

"Killing him won't, neither. Dead or alive, he'll be with you—till you get rid of this crazy hatred of yours."

"Ain't I got cause for it?"

"Plenty, more'n likely. I ain't sayin' you can't have an enemy—even levy justice on him—but not out of dumb hatred. You keep hating him, he wins."

He'd said much the same previous to this. But though I tried to savvy, I couldn't. Not when it come to Jack.

I said, "What do you mean by plenty, more'n likely?"

Noah turned aside. Him and the Dutchman looked at each other for the longest time, till I felt the blood start to rush in my ears.

I said, "What's this about?"

"I'll tell you something you didn't know." He picked up a stick in his one hand and worried the coals. "There was that morning back at the agency, when I was coming out of the fever. Opened my eyes and this little gal was by the side of my bed, along with this feller she called Nicaagat. I didn't rightly know where I was or who these two were, so I closed my eyes again and I listened."

I recalled it now. Later that morning I'd gone into the room to get my gun. That's when Noah warned me. He said to watch my step—that Josie liked Jack.

"Go on," I said.

"It was the dangedest thing, like nothing I'd ever heard. She had a way with this Indian like she might have had with a beau. And he talked to her—well, it was like he put her up on a pedestal. But it weren't for bein' a white woman. He was just lovesick, is all. And he told her so, right there. Nothing like you'd ever heard from an Indian. He told her there was two things in the world that he loved—the land and her. More than his people or his wives or his sons or his horses. He wanted her hand, plain and simple."

"What did she do?"

"She laughed. Prettiest little tinkly sound in the world. But if you're sweet on a girl, that laugh breaks your heart."

"Did she say anything?"

"She told him she had her ma and her pa to worry with, and that for the time being she couldn't marry anyone."

"That's all?"

"If you mean, did she let him know he was out of line—no. She made it sound like it was hard to turn him down."

I was on my feet. "That can't be true."

"Who's to say, Tory? That's how it sounded. But right now you ought to go talk to her. Maybe she can make you understand things."

"Why? What else am I gonna find out?"

"Wolf here thinks Jack took her for his squaw."

"Ouray said that didn't happen."

"Ouray said he was told it didn't happen. You can't blame him. He wouldn't want to be told if it did."

I caught the Dutchman's eye. "Is it true?"

His look said what I guess I already knew.

Noah said, "Wolf asked her. She denied it."

"Then why . . ."

"He knows these Indians. It would of been the thing for Jack to do. Point of pride."

I let the Dutchman know I wanted it straight from him. He fetched forth a piece of paper. He wrote slow and careful. All I could do was wait for him to finish. And while I did I saw things in my mind I could hardly bear.

What the note said was this—that for a chief to take a woman as his squaw is an honor. He would not see it as doing her harm. And if he didn't take her for himself, it would be like saying to the others that she was up for grabs. If he had feelings for Josie, he would've had to take her.

The Dutchman had writ one more thing at the bottom. "Try to think like a Ute."

I stood there and I thought, all right. I thought like a man whose sweetheart had been took by an Indian. Then I heard sounds coming from up the hill a ways, and I saw the very one. Wood Gettys was with him, and Ouray, and some of Ouray's cronies. They carried torches, and moved closer till they were at our fire and all their faces stood out against the darkness around us.

Gettys said, "Nicaagat here has made his choice."

CHAPTER 15

THE Dutchman motioned to them all to set round the fire. Then Ouray spoke. He said he could not free Nicaagat, even if Nicaagat were to win this fight. He said Nicaagat must face the white man's justice—which would be progress in itself and a better deal than Indians were used to getting. Ouray said that if Nicaagat could be set free, he'd have set him free in the first place—that the young chief had much cause to fight the cavalry at Milk Creek, and that the question of what had happened at White River was still open. But Ouray said there could be no breaking a pact he'd hammered out for the sake of his tribe, and Nicaagat had to understand that. If Nicaagat wished to fight this Nameless One, it would be for the sake of killing him, and nothing else.

Jack listened till Ouray was done, his eyes seeming to stare somewheres deep inside the fire. Then he spoke. He started off in Ute and Ouray held up his palm and said a few words. Then Jack went on in English, though he managed to talk to the Utes that were gathered there, and to the Dutchman, but not to me or Gettys or Noah. Jack said that he was not eager to go before a white man's court, and that when that came to pass he'd have nothing to say in his own defense. He said that the only judgment that meant a thing to him was that of Ouray and the other Utes. He said that the long knives had tried to take him in battle, but could not. To be forced to make bargains for him was their disgrace, and as their captive he would shame them further by the way he carried himself.

Then Jack said that even if he couldn't go free, he was thankful to Ouray just for the chance to kill the Nameless

One. Said this Nameless One had taken pleasure in Nathan Meeker's attempts to humiliate the Utes and had encouraged the cavalry to cross the reservation line at Milk Creek. And during the battle and later that night, he'd killed some of Jack's friends.

There were a lie or two hid in there, and one or two other things left out. But I didn't feel the need to speak, for I was rarin' to have my say through different means.

But Noah spoke up. "How about me, partner? I killed Sowerwick."

Jack answered without turning his head. "I do not fight women or one-armed men."

And Noah said, "You get by Tory, you'll fight this one."

I reckon Gettys could feel things getting out of hand. He asked Ouray what the rules would be.

The chief drew the knife from the beaded sheath at his waist. The blade caught the firelight—a gleaming thing it was with a slight curve to it. The handle was ribbed and looked to be ivory.

About twenty-five feet upstream from us, there stood a single white oak, lit spooky by the fire and the torches and the half-moon overhead. Ouray drew back his forearm and flicked the knife those twenty-five feet through the air and plumb into the center of the trunk, about eight foot off the ground.

He said a few words in Ute, and Shavano and Sapovanero, along with some other crony of his whose name I didn't know, got to their feet. They spread out to form three corners of a square, maybe twenty paces to a side. The white oak marked the fourth. Me and Jack were to stand in the far corner from the tree. At Ouray's signal we'd be free to go for the knife.

Me and my uncle moved off a few yards into the dark. Noah said, "You might want to get to that knife before he does."

"Good idea."

"You're quicker than he is. He's stronger. Get the knife. Use it quick. Don't get to wrasslin' with him."

Our eyes met. I said, "Somethin' happens, find Pa. That comes first."

"All right, son."

In the darkness among the trees on Plateau Creek, you could hear a thrush calling. It was a lovely sound. Right next to me, so close you could feel the heat coming off him, Jack crouched low.

I dug in too and bent my legs for to spring forward across the square.

Ouray clapped his hands.

I took two steps and Jack's forearm shot out and hit me across the face. As I fell I caught him round the ankles and took him down. But I wasn't gonna wrassle with him. I was up again and sprinting hard. He was just back of me. He lunged and I felt his fingers rake my shoulder but I had a step on him and was almost at the tree. I had to reach upward for the knife and as I stretched out my body and got my fingers up round the knife, Jack dove for my legs and drug me down. I tried to grasp the knife as I fell but all I got was the blade and it slit open the palm of my hand.

I didn't feel no pain at first, but when I got my hands up around Jack's throat the blood made it slick. I couldn't keep my grip and maybe I couldn't have even if I wasn't hurt, for his strength seemed twice mine and all at once I was on my back with him straddling my chest and punching my face. My hands were free and I got my forearms up to shield myself and help me twist out from under him. I made him lose his balance, and as I pushed up off the ground he fell sidewise and suddenly he was on the ground and I was standing, and I took one step toward the tree, got the knife in my hand, and fell upon him.

The pain in my hand didn't matter, and anyway I had the knife in both my hands and I was thrashing at him, thrashing like some kind of demon reared on hatred and fear, and as he struggled to get away, one of the thrusts of the knife caught him full in the thigh and he shrieked. When his leg recoiled, I lost my grip on the knife and Jack rolled away.

I sprung to my feet then, the breath whistling through my nostrils, every cord in my body aching to leap at him. But he was up now, too—dragging that leg up with him, the sweat pouring off his face, the look in his eyes like some wounded thing that knew it could die. His right hand reached down and yanked the knife out of his thigh, and the blood spurted after it. The hand drew back and he parried with the knife and then lunged, the knife slashing from his right to left. I pulled in my belly as the blade went by, and as he followed through I locked my hands together and laid a blow on the back of his shoulders. But that was where his strength lay— in his shoulders and back and chest—and whilst my body was extended in the blow he swung back and under my outstretched arms, both his hands grasping the knife, and slammed the butt of the handle into my side. It was the same spot where Sowerwick had stabbed me back at Milk Creek.

I went to my knees, seeing nothing, just craving breath. I couldn't lift my arms. My legs started to push up from where I knelt, but Jack was there again with the same fearsome blow, to my jaw this time. My head snapped back and I felt nothing anywhere, and then I was on the ground, laying on my side.

Come on, Tory, you lay here and you get killed. I twisted onto my belly and drug my knees up under me, but as I lifted my head I felt a hand shove my shoulder back into the dirt.

"It is not as you hoped, is it, Nameless One?"

I looked up at him squatting beside me. The mask was finally gone. I would have tried again to get up and fight him, but something told me he too was taking a breather. I had me a minute.

He set right down by my head, weary-like, the knife laying

on his knee, his left hand pressed to the wound in his thigh. The blood gleamed, and each time his heart beat, more seemed to well up through his fingers. I looked up at his face. It weren't hatred writ there—it was another thing, contempt.

He spoke again, soft-like so's only I could hear him. Around us I knew there were others, but they might have been miles off for all it meant to me and Jack.

"It should have been easy for you," he said. His breath come hard to him. "You who are young and fearless. To be white, in this time of the white man."

"I'm gonna get up soon, and I'm gonna kill you."

He laughed. A quick sort of laugh from back in his throat. "Do you know what is hardest, Nameless One? It is hardest to die when you do not respect the one that kills you. I learn this now."

I thought about that, laying there. I respected him. I'd spoke with him only a couple of times, but I hadn't needed to talk with him to hate him. But what I saw of him had also earned my respect, I'll confess to that. I would have wanted his respect as well.

He said, "Do you know why you hate me? You hate Nicaagat because Nicaagat is a man. This makes things hard for you. Nicaagat should vanish before you like smoke. But he stays, he is flesh. He will not disappear for you. He thinks against you with his mind, like a man. He fights you like a man. He takes your girl from you like a man. This is troublesome to you. You wish him just to go away. Other white men have this problem, Nameless One."

His eyes softened. He lifted his hand from off his leg and stared at the blood. And then as I watched, more baffled than I'd ever been, he slumped down beside me. I didn't think anymore about trying to best him. I didn't think at all before I spoke. I said, "You feel sorry for me."

He shook his head. "I feel nothing for you."

"You lie. You wouldn't have said all this if you didn't."

He said nothing. His head come to rest on the grass and his eyes shut.

I thought, he should hear me speak his name—his right name. I said, "Nicaagat."

His lids fluttered for a moment and there was that laugh again. He whispered, "Bowhunter," and he was dead.

Come first light a party formed up to take the Ute prisoners down off the mesa. There was Douglas and three others now—still enough so's justice might be served, and enough so's the cavalry would have a prize to show off at home. The Dutchman joined up with that bunch. He was of a mind to be with Douglas for a spell before that old friend was took away.

Josie and the others were to be taken southward. Ouray would guarantee their safety to Los Pinos. From there Gettys would take them to the railhead at Alamosa and then by train to Greeley. There'd be an inquest after that—in Denver, like as not. And then a trial for the Utes—no telling where. But in the meantime the town that Nathan Meeker had founded seemed the most fitting place for his widow and daughter.

Gettys explained that to me whilst we rode to the big camp to get the women and children. He drove the wagon and I set beside him. Noah rode alongside on the blue roan.

I said, "I'm wondering how she is."

"You'll find out directly," Gettys said.

"That's the girl that sawed off my arm," Noah said. "She'll be all right."

It was the second or third time someone had put it that way—but I wondered what it meant. Did being "all right" mean being "the same as before?" Do you ever stay the same?

It was half-past ten when we come into camp and whoaed up. I said, "Wood, I'm obliged for what you done."

"I ain't so sure I did you a favor."

"You done what was asked of you. It was all my doing—right or wrong."

"And which was it?"

"I spent the night thinking about it. I don't know."

Just then the flap lifted on the nearest tepee, and Josie come out.

Gettys said, "Maybe you'll know more in a little while."

My heart sped up at the sight of her—her hair in braids almost white from the sun, her face tanned and windburnt but so pretty that when I saw her I knew I was lost all over again. She had one of them Mexican shirts on that the Utes liked to wear, bright blue like a chicory flower.

She and I drove out alone to the edge of the mesa. I helped her down from the wagon and we stood on the rim overlooking the valley of Grand River. Across the valley was a line of gray and red sandstone bluffs—and then a hundred miles of broken desert that stretched away off into Utah.

Josie said, "That's where the Utes are headed."

She'd reasoned it through same as I had. Thanks to the killings at White River, the politicians in Denver had got what they needed. The Utes were as good as gone.

I tried to show some hope. "Might take a while," I said.

"What difference does it make if it's today or a year from now? Indians and whites see time in a different way. To Indians it's as if the future had already happened."

That was something to ponder. But Josie had always known these Indians better than any of us. Back at the agency she'd done more than just live among the Utes. She'd given her heart to them. They'd killed her pa and her friends and run off with her and her ma, but it was like she'd come to know them so well, to care about them so fierce, that she could not summon hatred.

I'd worried and wondered so long about her, and now that we were together it was like something remained between us—a distance I'd never cover. It's what kept me from taking her up in my arms.

Still I fretted for her. I said, "I like your braids. It's like you're an Indian maiden."

She just kept her eyes out on the bluffs over yonder. She hadn't smiled. I'd have given much to see her smile.

"Was it awful for you, Josie?"

She shook her head. "It wasn't the way you'd have imagined it."

"Were you scared?"

"For Mother I was. Jane wanted us killed. She kept prodding the men about it."

"But no harm was done you?"

She made no answer to that. She did say she'd been lonely a lot of the time. "The other squaws wouldn't have much to do with me or Flora Ellen. Douglas had to order them just to share food with us. They were jealous of us."

"Well, sure," I said. "Either one of you would make a right prettier squaw than any of them."

I hadn't meant nothing by that, but her eyes flashed at mine and then away. She was startled, like I'd hit on something.

Then I guessed it. The Ute squaws would have had cause to be jealous only if the white women had been treated real special. Real special meant they'd been taken as squaws by men of rank.

I said, "Who got Flora Ellen?"

"Loud Cry. His father didn't want her."

So it was true. The thought come to rest on me like stone. I squinted up at the sun. Be time to move on soon.

I said, "I reckon you heard about Nicaagat."

"I know he's dead." There was a chill in Josie's voice. "Ouray sent a runner."

When I spoke next I heard the same chill in mine. It surprised me. "I gotta know something, Josie. Gettys asked you about him—asked if he'd done anythin' to you. You said he hadn't."

"Hadn't what?"

"I don't want to say it."

"Say what?" she said. "They asked me if he'd 'committed an indignity' upon my person." She looked straight at me, chin held high. "It was not an indignity. It was what a Ute chief had to do. It was all dignity."

I cast about for something to say. I guess it was all writ on my face—hurt and wonderment. Something more, too—something that hadn't a shape yet.

She said, "If I'd told them about it, they would have hanged him." Then her voice lost its fire, like she didn't care anymore. "It doesn't matter. You killed him, anyway."

"I reckon he earned it," I said.

"Did he?"

"I reckon you don't think killing forty cavalrymen counts for nothin'. Or murdering your pa or the others at White River. Or what he done to you."

Her eyes met mine directly. "I'm all right."

I looked close at her. It was true. She was all right. She understood something about all those deaths that I never would. And what had happened to her belonged to her, not to me. What Josie Meeker believed, she believed all the way. I admired her. But mixed in with that was something new— or maybe it was something that had been there but was gone now. I just felt emptied of her, like what I'd saw previous was what I'd wanted to see. What was real was something far different.

I thought about chasing Jack down Coal Creek Canyon, and of wading into him and his bunch that night at the agency. I thought of trailing the Utes for two weeks over Roan Plateau, and of making Wood Gettys go against his conscience so I could tangle with Jack. And I thought about killing the Indian, getting lucky and cutting an artery in his thigh, and how maybe he'd deserved better.

And I started to laugh.

I thought, these days it's just one lesson after another.

"Let's get back, Josie," I said. "It's time I went and found Pa."

CHAPTER 16

WE were in the mountains to the north and east of Hahn's Peak. Pine forests lay all about, and the air was sharp with the smell of them. The Dutchman led us onto trails I doubt any other white men had ever seen. Had a feller the nerve to follow him ahorseback, along crumbling defiles that clung none-too-sure to the bare face of the mountains, he'd get where he was headed in about half the time. The problem was staying alive that long. One time we were edging along a ledge that climbed about straight up and was no wider than my horse. I remarked one or two times about the drop. The Dutchman whoaed up right there, stopping dead on that ledge with a thousand feet of emptiness hanging there on our side, and wrote me a note. It said not to fear falling upon the rocks below, for by the time a man hit the bottom he'd have long since starved to death.

We come onto Tourmaline from the south, along the valley floor. On the hillsides you could see the mining scars. The spring of '75 was when the rush had hit. It had started, Wolf said, with placer mining, but then the usual hordes moved in and started carving into the mountain. Whatever color there was, dried up right quick, and by late in the fall of that year Tourmaline had gone from about six hundred fifty residents to ten. Struck their tents and left—like they'd done in the other boomtowns, and like they would again.

But when hopes were running high hereabouts, and folks had cleared the spruce to dig their claims, they used the logs to raise one big building. It was just a heap of ashes now, and mixed in amongst the ashes was some bones and some rags and little else. The Dutchman sifted through some of it—

squatted there a long time he did—and shook his head. There were depths to that man I'd not begun to fathom—I come to know I wasn't prepared to, due to being nineteen and having seen much less of living than he had. But it was like him, only because it was so surprising, and he was full of surprises, that he went to his saddlebags right then and fetched out a raggedy old volume of something writ by another Dutchman, name of Goethe. He riffled through it till he got to the right place and pointed out what I should read.

I took it up and read it out loud. What this Goethe said was that men who grow too certain of their own righteousness can do evil and call it good.

I reflected on that. It seemed I'd come across just such a case back at White River—though why the Dutchman chose just now to point it out I didn't rightly know.

In truth, I was past reflecting. I'd had about ten days' worth of it on the trail since cutting loose of Josie and Gettys and Sensibaugh and every other thing that had tied me to White River. Right now we were getting close to where the Dutchman had last seen Pa, and I was working at putting the rest behind me. We'd traveled light and fast those warm autumn days—knowing the good weather couldn't last—and finally it looked like, if we were gonna find him at all, it would be today.

We nooned at Tourmaline, but we made quick work of it and ate our beans cold. There wasn't much talk. It was a spooky place, and when we got away from there I was glad of it. We spurred the horses further up the valley. In a few miles the valley curled round to the left and then narrowed considerable as we clumb higher. There were canyons and smaller ravines, some pretty wild and spooky in their own right, entering the valley from either side, and as the walls of the valley growed more steep, you hardly knew where each one come in until you were looking into it.

Noah said, "If we'd of tried to find your pa hereabouts, by now they'd be lookin' for us."

I turned to the Dutchman and said, "Can you really tell one of these from the next?"

He smiled by way of saying yes. I'd growed used to that smile—he'd learned to pack a lot of meaning into it—and by now I could read it. This time it held something dark inside it—like something troubled him, but he wasn't about to say what.

Directly I asked him, "Why did you split off from Pa?"

He made two motions with his hands. One was like he was digging with a shovel. The next was palms up—empty.

Noah said, "That's simple enough."

Simple enough. But as the Dutchman swung round to face ahead, I thought, There's something more here—something left unspoken.

Whilst we rode that afternoon, the wind hove around from the north and the clouds rolled in. I could feel the change on the back of my neck.

"Mite brisk," I said.

Noah studied the clouds. " 'Bout time, I'd say."

What we were both thinking was that it had been hot this morning and might snow tonight.

I'd had my fill of these parts. There are men made for living in the wild places. The Dutchman, for one. He was a man with book learning, born and bred among crowds of folks—and he'd picked this sort of country to make his life. But I felt different toward it. It give me a sad and hollow feeling—the air too whispy to fill your chest, the sight of far-off peaks as beautiful as a dream, but with nothing to make you feel part and parcel of it. Up here was real lonesomeness. And hard by, these ravines—each one wild, almost haunted. There was no home here for me.

We come onto one canyon that was just like all the rest, save for a big old limber pine that marked the opening. It was just a tough, gnarled old tree that had anchored itself to the rocks some centuries prior to this and wasn't about to let go—even if there didn't appear to be nothing for it to grow on but gravel and air. The Dutchman pointed out a bunch of notches carved into the bark. The notches formed the letters MB.

He took out his paper and his writing tool and wrote me a note. It said for me and Noah to head on up this canyon till there weren't nothing left of it—and there we ought to find Pa. No more than a mile, it said. Two at most.

What was happening sunk in on Noah quicker than me. He said, "And where are you off to?"

The Dutchman pointed back the way we come.

"Why?" I said, almost laughing at the suddenness of it. "You can't."

Once more that smile crossed his face. It was funny, those merry eyes and red cheeks—but with steel underneath. I knew there was no turning him.

I said, "Just tell me why."

He wrote it out. *I have seen enough craziness lately. This I will leave to you.*

I couldn't guess at what he meant, but I knowed better than to crowd him. He was gonna get back to living the way he'd chose. I shook his hand and said good-bye to him. He give Uncle Noah a nod and reined about, and as he rode out of sight I wondered if old Goethe would have knowed what to make of him.

"We'd best get to it," Noah said.

We stepped our horses round that old devil limber pine and up into the canyon. Five years was long enough to wait to see your pa.

The wash give us a good wide path to ride, so the way was easy. Off the main canyon, though, there was other draws to look into—mostly choked with thickets and broken rock. We scouted each one. Some stretched far back into the folds of

the mountain. It was tangled ground, easy to lose yourself—
or anything else you had a mind to.

The gloom hung thick hereabouts, the sun lost somewheres behind the mass of gray clouds, the wind picking up
so's you could hear it in the rocks. I got to feeling like we'd
come to the edge of the world.

And there was Pa.

He called down from the rim above our right shoulder,
holding his Winchester in one hand and waving with the
other. I shouted halloo and waved back at him and in a
minute or two we were shaking hands at the base of the
canyon wall.

Me and Pa just sort of studied each other and grinned.
Didn't seem like neither of us knew what to say.

But Noah said, "Well, brother, you're in one piece."

"Never been better," Pa said. He turned back my way.
"Tory boy—just look at you. What brings you here?"

"Why, you sent for me, Pa."

For just a fraction there he looked puzzled. "Well, you
wouldn't be here if I hadn't."

Noah's eye caught mine. A question flickered between us.
I said, "I know it took us a while to get here, Pa, but we come
a distance."

"No matter, boy, got something for you to see."

"Wolf Miller led us here . . ."

His look sort of darkened. "He's still hereabouts?"

I shook my head. "Had other business."

"He didn't tell you nothin'?"

Noah said, "No. Said that if you had something to tell us,
it was yours to do."

"Good man," Pa said. "Keeps his word. Come on now—we
still got us some daylight."

As he turned about and we begun to follow with the horses,
he caught sight of the buffalo tail that hung from my belt. I
saw him stop at the sight of it, and I smiled.

"I still got it, Pa."

"Get rid of that thing." His voice was deadly cold.

He'd been five years in the mountains and looked no worse for it. Fact, he looked better than I remembered him—lean and leathery-skinned, his eyes just two glittery blue points set deep under his brows. But his eyes kept jumping around, like he was looking out for something bad to happen, not knowing where it was gonna come from but knowing that it would come regardless. It wasn't just the wariness of a man who lives out of doors. It was like a man pursued by something.

He led us further up the canyon, till the walls become craggier on both sides and veered off sharp to the right and the climb grew steeper.

"I expect you're the only one ever come this way," I said.

"It'll surprise you," he said. "A man can come right over the other side of the mountain and drive a wagon in here. Thing is, you gotta start off on the other side of the mountain."

I asked him what was on the other side, and he said the town of Chastine lay twenty miles distant, down in North Park. Not much of a town, not much more than Tourmaline had been, but a farming town, more likely to last.

Noah said, "Had much Indian trouble thereabouts?"

"Not that I heard," Pa said.

"We heard tell of the Utes settin' forest fires all about to scare off the settlers."

Pa kind of grunted. "Any fool knows the weather's been dry. Folks just want to believe it's Indians."

"Well, then," Noah said, "what about Tourmaline?"

"Just like I said."

Another riddle.

We come onto a fork in the ravine and headed up the steeper path. The way looked clear enough, but fifty yards in front of us you could see it twisted round to the left and out of sight.

"Tie the horses," Pa said.

We done like he told us and ventured on afoot.

I said, "You come this way with the Dutchman?"

"Yep. 'Cept he cut out. Didn't know value."

I felt my heart start to beat. "Then you did find something."

"Sure."

"Gold?"

"Better than that, Tory."

Noah said, "Silver ain't better'n gold."

"Didn't say it was. Didn't say nothin' about silver."

I said, "Then what is it?" I was tiring of riddles.

"This is what it is, boy."

We'd just rounded a bend in the ravine and off on the right there was one more narrow opening.

I heard myself say, "Jesus."

It was the mouth of a draw bordered on three sides by towering hills—a wondrous grassy place tucked into the flank of the mountain, with a spring that flowed forth from one of the hills to form a deep-blue pond. There were wildflowers of the same color scattered through the grass. And browsing in that meadow, not moving a whole lot, and making no sound, more like a vision you had just conjured up in your mind than something really there, were seventy, maybe eighty head of buffaloes.

Pa said, "These here are my babies."

After a spell Noah said, "We best move aside. They stampede, they come this way."

Pa shook his head. "They ain't gonna stampede. They've nothin' to run from. Not up here."

I said, "How'd it happen, Pa? What're they doing here?"

"Dunno, Tory. Don't know how they got here. But what they're doin' is, they're surviving."

Noah said he'd heard about such critters a time or two. "They call them mountain buffalo. They might've bred up here or they might just of strayed westward ahead of the hunters till they got out of reach—nobody knows. But your pa's right. They're alive whilst most all the rest are dead."

I glanced over Pa's way. He was listening with half an ear. Mostly he was gazing upon the herd.

"Is this why you sent for me, Pa? This what you found?"

He nodded, just barely. "Wanted you to see. When I found 'em last spring, I didn't know if I'd have to fight to keep folks off. Thought I might need your help more'n I have." He looked me in the eye. "You ain't sorry, are you?"

I didn't know. I was caught up in too many thoughts.

Noah said, "You're the only one knows of this?"

"Just about. The Dutchman was with me. One other feller fetched up here out of North Park, maybe a week or ten days ago. Friend of yours—said he'd heard I needed help." Pa grunted again. I guess it was what he did by way of laughter. "He thought I'd found gold. Must have asked me about it fifty different ways. Took me for a fool."

"Have a name?" I asked, though of course I knew.

"Dunno. Didn't much care. Said he was headin' back, but he trailed me here and saw the herd. Then I shooed him off proper." He run his hand along the barrel of his Winchester. "He won't be back."

You had to hand it to Bill Nunan. He'd set out to find Pa, and that's what he did. But you had to laugh, too—all that fussin' and deception over nothing. Nothing but the sight of some big woolly critters that it used to be you could see anytime.

"Come on," Pa said. "Show you something."

"I think I'll stay put," Noah said.

Pa laid down his Winchester—had me do the same—and me and him walked out amongst the herd. I wasn't real eager to do this, but Pa waved me along. The buffalo didn't pay us much mind. The bulls were taller than I was and a good ten feet long. Pa just kinda talked low to them and they went on cropping grass. If one stood in Pa's way, he give it a little shove alongside the shoulder and it would move aside for him.

It was said that old Bill Cody used to step up and shoot them in the ear with a pistol. The fact they were so dumb and trusting is what cost them their lives. Maybe it wasn't dumb and trusting. Maybe it was just dumb and stubborn—like they figured it was their ground no less than yours and by God they'd hold it. Then they'd get killed and be cut up for rugs.

They had nought to fear from Pa, though. He petted them like they were children, and whilst he did that he explained to me that he was a happy man. He'd found out what it was he needed to do. He was gonna watch over these beasts, keep them from harm. He'd been doing it for six months now and he felt pretty good about it.

I said, "It ain't tiresome, though? And lonesome?"

"Lonesome? Back in the spring I had me sixty-one of these critters. Now I got eighty-one. Gettin' more company all the time."

"But people—don't you miss having folks around?"

He didn't answer right off. But I couldn't be sure he was listening. Sometimes when it seemed he'd finished saying something, you'd start to speak and he'd keep muttering to himself. All the while them eyes of his went darting everywhere, restless.

I said, "Pa, I recall some good times we had."

He said, "People are a disease. One is too many. More'n that is a plague that needs to be scoured out!"

His voice rose so that the calf he'd been petting snorted and swung its shoulders about. I heard Noah call out a warning from yonder by the mouth of the draw. I reckon I just stood amazed—I knew now what the Dutchman had meant when he wrote out his good-bye.

"Sun's goin' down," Pa said. He sounded all right again. "My camp ain't far distant."

We went and fetched the horses. Noah'd brung whiskey in his war bag. Pa said as how he hadn't seen much of that lately. I guess Noah was feeling tender and give him the bottle.

Pa did a lot of talking whilst he drank. Plenty of words—though they didn't add up to much more than that buffaloes were good critters and worth more than all of humanity taken together. He said he had come out here from Kansas to prospect for gold. Him and the Dutchman had been up and down this range together. They'd found no gold, but they'd learned many a lesson concerning greed and thievery.

"Ain't nothing lower than a prospector," he said. He was staring into the fire. "Can't even touch one or you'll get it on your hands."

"What are you talkin' about?" Noah said.

Pa said, "What was I sayin'?"

My uncle's eyes caught mine again. I didn't know what had come over Pa but it was a scary thing. His home was a cave. It was good shelter but it was a place for a man to make camp, not to live. The fire throwed our shadows up on the wall. Outside the wind gusted cold. I thought, Come morning we'd best leave here.

"You know, Pa," I said. "What with all these Indian troubles, maybe we ought to winter down in North Park. Chastine ain't far from here."

He shook his head. "I told you, boy, there ain't been no Indian problems." He leaned a mite closer, like he was fixing to share a secret with me. "It just serves to have folks think there are."

I could feel Noah move out along the wire edge. He said, "Tell me more about that, brother."

Pa leaned back again like he'd captured himself an audience and would be right pleased now to entertain it. He took a pull on the bottle.

"For instance," he said. "Month or two back, next valley over. I'm on one side of the valley, and on the other, where the old Ute hunting trail runs by—I see a fire. Too far to make out faces—my eyes ain't what they once was, no how. But the one thing I know certain is that I don't need no company. So I hunker down there behind the rocks and throw some lead their way. First shot—first shot, now—whap! Hits right in the camp fire. Coals flyin' everywhere. Best piece of shooting I done since my killing days."

Me and Noah were still. Pa's eyes went back and forth between us, the fire glowing in them.

"Well," he said. "They scattered right quick—three or four of 'em there was. Smothered the fire, didn't leave me much of a target. But I just kept a'throwin' lead—changing off with the guns I had so they'd think there was more'n one of me. See, the intention was to make 'em think it was Indians— kind of make 'em eager to go back the way they come in."

"It worked," Noah said.

"Sure did," Pa said, excited. "But that wasn't all. One way or 'nother, the brush catches fire o'er yonder and they're running for cover like ants. One of 'em, though, he puts on quite a show for me—blastin' from the hip, like that'll scare me off. Come close to fallin' off the mountain, I was laughin' so hard."

He grunted again and took another swallow. " 'Course, next morning they was gone. Lit a shuck out of there— probably off to tell half of Colorado how the Utes were on the prod and how white folks had best keep away."

I said, "Pa, that was . . ."

"Wait, Tory," Noah said. Pa got quiet. He just set there, those eyes so spooky.

Real casual-like, Noah said, "I was just wonderin', Micah. Them fellers you scared off like that—what did you think they were up to?"

Pa's back arched just a hair. "Why, it don't matter none what they was up to. They was here. It's my place to keep 'em away."

"From your babies?"

"I knew you'd savvy." He tapped his finger against the side of his head. "Blood'll tell."

Noah said, real quiet, "Is that why you burned 'em out at Tourmaline?"

"Same reason. Folks were makin' noises like there was color turnin' up again. Word of that gets out, and you're swamped with miners and every variety of riffraff, and then they're into every gully and ravine for miles about and before you know it they've found my babies."

The silence hung there a spell. I said, "Pa, there were *people* in that town."

"There's people everywhere," he said. "Fewer buffaloes."

Noah said, "You did it at night, when they were sleeping?"

Pa nodded. "One or two run out and I had to shoot 'em." He made a little gun with his thumb and forefinger. "Nothin' to it."

It was a distance both of us had come, him and me. I can't say why, but I thought then of open spaces—of the sky over Kansas where we'd hunted together, and the sky over Colorado where I'd gone to find him. I'd gone searching for one man and found another. I thought of nights we'd bedded down together when I was a boy, and how afterward, even when he wasn't there and I didn't know just where he might be, I could read stories about him in a book. It was like he was around, in a way. Now I'd found him and we were back together and it was harsh country. We were hunched around a flickery fire in a cave where the wind howled outside and ghosts walked—ghosts of folks killed for no reason but that the demons in Pa's head made it so.

I don't know how long I set there, just pondering that, but when I looked over at Pa he was passed out.

I said, "What are we gonna do, Noah?"

He shrugged. "You tell me, son. He says blood'll tell."

That's what it come down to. Noah was his brother but I was his son. It was mine to decide.

I got to my feet and went outside to check the horses. The wind was wild out of the north. There were no stars.

I reckoned it this way. We couldn't stay put with winter moving in. But we couldn't take Pa with us, for he just wouldn't go. And we couldn't leave him, for like as not he'd kill other folks.

I couldn't decide.

I slept fitful—waking once in a sweat, not knowing where I was—and when it come time to rouse myself I was glad of it. I rolled up my blanket and strapped on my Colt and clapped the leather to my horse even before I got Noah's coffee into me. I just wanted us out of there.

The sky was what decided it. The cloud cover was down amongst the treetops, like a great dark cloak fallen on us. I knew little of the ways of nature hereabouts but I reckoned I knew snow when I saw it coming. I ducked back inside.

"Uncle," I said, "I ain't eager to spend the winter in this here cave."

"Feel much the same, Tory boy. Which way are we headed?"

"Into North Park. It beats waitin' to get snowed in up here."

Pa come up from out of the dark. "You can be down into the park by suppertime. Chastine is no more'n twenty miles' ride after that."

I said, "I want you with us, Pa."

He shook his head. "I'm needed here."

Noah said, "Listen, brother. Seems to me them buffaloes found their way up here by their ownself. They'll live or die the same way. If the Lord's amind to, he'll provide for 'em."

Pa smiled. "He provided for 'em. He provided me."

Plain to say there wasn't much we could do against that line of thought. I remembered that book the Dutchman had me read out of. It said a man could be so sure of his own righteousness, he could do evil and call it good. If you lived long enough, you got to see it happen more than once.

There was no waste of words after that. Pa was a full-growed man. If he was amind to stay here, we'd no choice but to let him. Chances were that he couldn't do much harm, as no one else would ride this way in wintertime. In the spring me and Noah could come back. Maybe there'd be a change in Pa and we could talk sense again.

Then a shot sounded.

We listened, but inside the cave you couldn't tell distance or direction. The second shot echoed somewheres out yonder, and Pa grabbed his Winchester and bolted out of there.

At the mouth of the cave, where the horses were, Noah got his rifle from off his saddle, and in that moment I saw Pa scramble down the slope and then round the spur of the hill and out of sight. Another shot rung from off thataways—far too distant to be meant for us—and before the echo died out we tore off after Pa.

It was no more than a quarter-mile to the open end of the draw where the buffaloes were. And it was no trouble catching up with Pa, for when he'd got there he'd come to a halt. I could see him from the side as I run up to him, the thin air burning in my lungs. He looked like something carven out of rock.

What he'd caught sight of was a man on the closed end of the draw—maybe three hundred yards distant from us and halfway up the steep hillside. The feller had set himself in amongst the rocks, his foot braced on a dwarf cedar that growed out from a crevice. He was using his knee to steady his sights.

He was killing Pa's herd.

The way I guess Bill Nunan had it figured, there might not be any gold hereabouts, but there might still be a few coins to be had in the buffalo trade. Winter was late but it was coming. Folks down in Chastine might like to store up some buffalo tongue and some hump meat. Might pay pretty fair for it. There was no way Bill could skin his kill single-handed, but some simple butchering wouldn't be no problem.

The first time he'd been up here, Pa'd run him off. Nunan must have gone back down to Chastine, rustled up a wagon and a bigger gun—a single-shot Springfield by the sound of it—and now he was back.

Me and Pa stood there long enough so's Bill caught sight of us. He stopped, considering things. He made as if to wave his hat, but I guess he caught a whiff of Pa's intent. He swung the barrel around as a caution.

Pa mumbled something. "For money."

"Pa?"

"For money," he said again. He was coming unfroze from what he'd seen. He said it one more time—only now he started to run for the man who was killing his babies—and he made of the words a long fearsome howl.

He run like he feared not for his life nor nothing else. All he wanted was to kill this man. I think Bill froze for a spell, just in wonderment. But when Pa had covered half the distance and raised his gun to fire, Bill let him have it and Pa spun around and fell. I started to run to him and I heard another shot from over my shoulder and knew it was Noah. Pa got to his knees and I heard myself call out to him, and then he fired twice at Bill from the hip. But on the second shot Bill's rifle blazed again and Pa flew backwards. In a moment I was past him and then I was at the base of the hillside. I could see Bill fumbling with another cartridge. I used my hands and my feet and got myself up the slope, and as Bill swung the rifle in my direction I saw the panic come into his eyes. I drew my Colt. The buffalo gun boomed in my ears but by then Bill knew he'd never kill me. He twisted away as if to make himself small and I fired once into the side of his chest. That bullet left him upright, but my second one blew him clear off the rocks and he bounced twice before he hit the bottom.

Noah was with Pa. One shot had gone clean through Pa's shoulder. The other had tore up his hip.

Noah said to him, soft, "You stop bleedin' for us, and you'll live."

Pa's eyes were different now.

I said, "We're gonna get you down off of here."

He rolled his head over to the side so's he could see his buffaloes. The snow was falling now, and it dusted their hides.

"You know what, Pa? I plumb forgot. I brung you a letter. Let me read it for you."

I'd long since lost it, of course. But I knew enough of Sarie Clement to know what she would have writ.

"She says you got a place to go, Pa. She says she wants to take care of you. Would you like that, Pa? Can I take you there?"

"The snow," he said. Each word come hard. "They'll be snowed in."

He was right, of course. I reckon the seasons had fooled them, and they'd tarried too long in high pasture. Any sort of drifting snow and they'd be sealed up here for the winter.

I wondered if there was something to do. But I knew that if our gunfire hadn't stirred them to move, nothing else would. A person could do only so much. Buffaloes do what they want.

"If He's amind, God'll provide," Noah said. "We'd best fetch the horses."

I did. Then we got ourselves mounted—me and my one-armed uncle and my crazy pa—and we come down off that mountain.

POSTSCRIPT

BOWHUNTER is fiction, but in general outline its depiction of the events at White River in the fall of 1879 is true. The Utes did kill Nathan Meeker and the Greeley boys and did kidnap his wife, daughter Josie, and Flora Ellen Price and her children. All were freed through the intercession of Ouray, who died of Bright's disease soon afterward.

The following year, with the Meeker incident and the defeat at Milk Creek as the main pretext, the U.S. Army herded the Utes out of Colorado and into Utah.

History notwithstanding, in writing *Bowhunter* I have generally wrought havoc with what really happened. For the facts, I recommend, and recognize my extensive indebtedness to, Marshall Sprague's *Massacre: The Tragedy at White River*.

IF you have enjoyed this book and would like to receive details of other Walker Western titles, please write to:

Western Editor
Walker and Company
720 Fifth Avenue
New York, NY 10019